A dogged curiosity . . .

Her voice trailing behind me, I made my way through the gate and across the paddock, Sheba and Major romping ahead. Reaching the doghouse they stopped, sniffed around and started to whimper, alerting me to trouble even before the stomach-wrenching odour reached my nostrils. I braced myself. This was not going to be pleasant.

Cautiously I raised the burlap flap tacked across the entrance, disturbing a cloud of flies as I did so. Was my assignment to be over before it had fairly begun?

I was right. Definitely dead. But definitely not Herbie.

I'm not one to scream, but I admit I've never been closer to it. The sound that emerged from my throat was more of a shuddering gasp . . .

First in an all-new series featuring pet detective

Delilah Doolittle!

Delilah Doolittle

AND THE

Purloined
Pooch

Patricia Guiver

BERKLEY PRIME CRIME, NEW YORK

DELILAH DOOLITTLE AND THE PURLOINED POOCH

A Berkley Prime Crime Book / published by arrangement with
the author

PRINTING HISTORY
Berkley Prime Crime edition / October 1997

The Putnam Berkley World Wide Web site address is
http://www.berkley.com

ISBN: 0-425-15963-9

Berkley Prime Crime Books are published
by The Berkley Publishing Group,
a member of Penguin Putnam Inc.,
200 Madison Avenue, New York, NY 10016.
The name BERKLEY PRIME CRIME and the BERKLEY PRIME CRIME
design are trademarks belonging to Berkley Publishing Corporation.

PRINTED IN THE UNITED STATES OF AMERICA

10 9 8 7 6 5 4 3 2 1

To dear Brandy, my Dobie. The inspiration for Watson.

and

To my friend Chamois, a most elegant cockerpoo.
His ancestry may have been unclear, but there
was never any doubt of his good breeding.

Acknowledgments

Thanks to my many friends in the animal welfare field—professional, hobbyist, and volunteer—for their insights into their special realms. I particularly want to thank Dr. Todd Kopit, of the Stanton Pet Hospital, and Jack Edwards, retired director of the Orange County Animal Shelter, for so willingly sharing their knowledge and expertise. Also Tonya Ehrman for her thoughtful advice on animal behaviour.

Most of all I wish to thank the members of Patricia Mc-Fall's mystery writers' critique group, without whose encouragement and support this book would never have been written.

DISCLAIMER

No animals were harmed in the writing of this book.

Delilah Doolittle

AND THE

Purloined Pooch

· 1 ·

Delilah Gets a Call

"OH, NO, WATSON. Not again!" I said in dismay, as the big red Doberman pinscher sat down in the middle of the driveway and began to scratch.

Surf City dogs are different from dogs of my acquaintance elsewhere. They have more fleas. Something for which, along with mud slides and earthquakes, I had been totally unprepared when I first arrived in southern California from England some twenty-five years ago. This summer, as every year since then, by dint of much vacuuming, spraying, and cursing, we fought the battle of the fleas to a draw. And now, just when I thought I had the little blighters under control, here was Watson scratching again.

"You must have picked it up at the last shelter we visited," I said to her as I unlocked the front door. "One of the hazards of the pet detective's trade, I suppose. Well, it's bath time for you, old girl. We'll get it over with before dinner."

Watson, cowering at the threat, hastily pushed past me and ran for cover under the kitchen table.

I didn't look forward to the chore any more than she did. At my age (let's just say the shady side of fifty-five) and at five foot one, seven and a half stone, I'm no match for a damp and determined Doberman.

We need not have worried. The insistent ringing of the telephone which greeted me as I entered the house put all thoughts of fleas and baths out of my head.

At first I was inclined to let the answering machine pick up the message. After spending a hot September afternoon searching animal shelters for a delinquent poodle, I had been debating whether it would take a cup of tea or a gin and tonic to revive me, and was in no mood to chat. After all, if I'd come in five minutes later, I'd have missed the call, I rationalized. But fiscal necessity overcame rationalization. It might be a job: the poodle had been gone for more than a week this time, and the trail was getting cold. The mortgage payment was due on Friday. I was in no position to let work slide by.

"Delilah Doolittle, tracer of missing pets," I answered in as businesslike a manner as my parched mouth would allow.

"I can't find Herbie." The woman's sharp, clipped voice, though assertive, betrayed a hint of nervousness.

"Herbie being?"

"My German shepherd, Champion Herbert Fitzherbert. He's going to win best of breed at Westminster next year," the clipped voice replied proudly, referring to the Academy Awards of dogdom, held annually at New York's Madison Square Garden. "Herbie's his call name." Her tone implied that no further explanation was necessary.

It would have to be tea. Cradling the phone under my chin while I put on the kettle, and taking two Red Rose tea bags from the caddy, I reached for my notebook and proceeded to get details. Name—Mrs. Jessica Lomax, address—Orange Blossom Heights, telephone number, and a complete description of the dog who, aristocrat though he was, had apparently decided to go slumming. German shepherd, male, unneutered, six years old, black and tan.

"Last seen?"

Mrs. Lomax hesitated. "About a week ago."

This seemed a trifle careless for the loss of any pet, never mind a grand champion, and I'm afraid I was unable to hide my disapproval. "A week!" I said. "And you're only just reporting him missing?"

"I've been out of town, judging a dog show in San Diego," she explained. "I left Herbie, two other dogs, and two cats in the care of a pet sitter. I arrived home a few hours ago, and there's no sign of him or of Herbie."

"And your other pets?"

"All present and accounted for, though the cats' litter box is a disgrace, the dog run hasn't been picked up for days by the looks of it, and my other dogs are ravenous."

Obviously there had been some neglect on the part of the pet sitter, in whose shoes I would not like to be when this lady got through with him. From her voice I pictured Mrs. Lomax as a thin, grey-haired, sharp-featured martinet. My knowledge of dog shows was limited, but it was safe to assume that the years of experience necessary to become a show judge would make her at least fifty. I couldn't quite place the accent. New England, possibly.

She must have been thinking along the same lines, for she said, "Is that an Australian accent I detect?"

I bristled. Neither the English nor the Australians appreciate being mistaken for each other. And I'm not the one with the accent. But it's a common mistake, so I merely gave her my standard, "No, it's the Queen's English," in my most amiable tone, then quickly shifted the conversation back to the subject at hand, the missing Herbie.

"Were all three dogs supposed to be confined to the dog run while you were away?" I was wondering why they hadn't all taken off when the opportunity presented itself.

"Yes. That's the strangest thing. I left strict instructions that they were to be kept in the run except for exercising in the paddock. When I got home only Major and Sheba were there. The run was padlocked, but Herbie was gone."

"Have you tried contacting the sitter?"

"I've left a message on the answering machine. He's usually in the field or the kennels at this time of the day," she replied, going on to explain that the pet-sitting service was a sideline of a dog training and kennel business. The owner, Jim Ratchett, had promised that he would personally handle the job. "Herbie needs a firm hand, he can be a little difficult sometimes," she added in an indulgent tone.

Great. A recalcitrant German shepherd. I hoped I wasn't in for a repeat of the time I'd had to chase a shy collie around a city park, wielding my catch-pole like a cowboy trying to lasso a reluctant calf, all the while hindered by a couple of small boys who had delighted in their efforts to frustrate the "dogcatcher."

"One other thing," I asked. "Was Herbie wearing any form of identification? A license or personal ID tag?"

Again she hesitated. "No. Herbie would never run away. And anyone stealing him would remove a tag immediately. Besides," she went on, "he's a show dog. A collar would rub a mark in his neck fur."

I sighed. Show people were exasperating. They paid the earth for their dogs, spent a fortune on the show circuit, but refused to see the wisdom of protecting their investment with a five-dollar ID tag.

"A tattoo, anything?" I persisted.

"I told you, nothing." She was getting irritated with me. But the more information I have, the better I can do my job.

While talking I leafed through my notes for the day. At the six southland shelters I had visited, I had noted several German shepherds, though only a couple of them had looked even remotely like the champ Mrs. Lomax described, and their pickup point was nowhere near her home in Orange Blossom Heights.

I informed her of my terms: $75 a day, plus expenses (for flyers, posters, classified ads, out-of-town travel), with a $100 nonrefundable deposit payable when she signed the contract. In return, she would get a weekly report and, with any luck, the return of her pet. I usually adjusted my fee according to the client's ability to pay. Mrs. Lomax would obviously be willing to shell out quite a bit for the return of Herbert Fitzherbert, which would make up for the occasions when I didn't have the heart to charge a senior citizen on a fixed income for finding a cherished companion.

"Travel expenses?" Mrs. Lomax was saying. "Surely you don't think he could have left the area?"

Oh, dear, I thought. I shouldn't have said that. Now she might worry needlessly. But there was always the possibility that the dog might have been picked up by someone with the best, or perhaps the worst, of intentions, and then escaped from them somewhere out of town. Then our only hope would be that he would be taken to a local shelter and we could track him down there. To cover this contingency I made weekly calls to all shelters in the southern California area, and circulated flyers to shelters throughout the western states.

Having been assured that an out-of-town trip wasn't very likely, we just needed to cover every eventuality, Mrs. Lomax readily agreed to my terms.

"Please find him before he gets picked up by animal control," she said. "I don't want him to go to the pound."

I told her that in my opinion going to the animal shelter was not the worst thing that could happen to a lost pet. He'd be taken care of, fed, and kept out of harm's way until his owner claimed him.

"No. That would be too traumatic for him," Mrs. Lomax replied. "He's not used to places like that. I'm counting on you to find him before he gets there. That's why I'm engaging your services. If you don't want the job, I'll get someone else."

I refrained from pointing out that, as far as I knew, the telephone yellow pages were not exactly brimming with pet detective listings. Few people would consider traipsing around animal shelters looking for errant canines a desirable occupation. Some might even consider it a trifle eccentric. Certainly it was not a job from which fortunes were to be made. But tracing lost pets is what I do, and I think that most of the time I do it rather well. Though if I'd had any idea of the trouble my search for Herbie was to get me into, this was one assignment I would have graciously declined.

But at this point all I knew was that if I wanted the job there was no point in annoying Mrs. Lomax any further. So, saying something reassuring about how I was sure Herbie would soon show up, and that I would see her sometime within the hour, depending on traffic, I hung up.

I had said "weekly" reports, but seldom did cases take longer than a week, a fortnight at the most. The trail of a missing pet, like that of a missing person, gets cold very quickly. One has to act fast while memories are still fresh. While I always advise owners "never give up," and routinely keep the pets on my active list and continue to look for them when I do my shelter rounds, in my experience the chances of finding a lost pet diminish with each passing day. They usually show up in the first few hours or days or not at all. There are exceptions, of course. Like the case of the Pekingese who had been left in a car stolen from a parking lot at a local amusement park. The car had never been recovered, as far as I knew, but little Lulu had shown up three months later performing in a magic act in Las Vegas. That had been my first and, in many respects, my most successful case. But it was also one of the more unusual, considering the time and distance involved.

Herbie had already been gone several days, possibly a week. There was no time to lose.

I looked at the clock. Half past three. It would take me at least twenty minutes to get from my Surf City beach home to Mrs. Lomax's place. If I left right now I might get a jump on the rush hour exodus, and the sooner I started, the better for all—Jessica Lomax, Herbie, and me and my bank account.

Better shower and change first, though. It would hardly do to show up smelling of eau de kennel for my first encounter with a new client. Chasing dogs (it's usually dogs; cat owners tend to rely on the old adage "he'll come home when he's hungry," and by the time they sound the alarm, it's too late) demanded serviceable and comfortable attire. Though some might consider tee shirts and jeans a little too youthful for a woman of my vintage, my small build allowed me to get away with it. ("If you've got it, flaunt it," my friend Evie always says.) But for this afternoon's meeting I decided my tan cotton pantsuit with cream silk shell would be more appropriate.

I gulped down the last of my tea and checked the answering machine. A call from Mrs. Jones, tearfully inquiring about the poodle. Mrs. Jones was a bread-and-butter client. Her dog Tasha was a regular escape artist who ran away at least three or four times a year, but Mrs. Jones still couldn't be persuaded to fix her fence. The dog usually showed up at the local shelter within a couple of days, but this time I was beginning to suspect the worst, maybe she'd been run over or stolen. I would put off calling Mrs. Jones as long as possible.

Two calls from Evie, my friend in San Diego.

"Dee, are you there? You know how I hate leaving messages on this tiresome machine. Call me the minute you get in."

On the second call, with her impatience ratcheting up a notch or two, Evie's upper-class English accent became more pronounced. *"Dee, you really are the limit. What can you be doing all this time? It is imperative that I speak to you straight away."*

Everything was imperative to Evie. Yet sometimes I would listen to her waffle on for an hour or more, never getting a word in edgewise, and still be none the wiser as to why she had called. She just loved to chat. Enjoyable, yes, but I had no time for that right now.

Watson, sensing that the threatened bath was no longer

imminent, was now splayed out on the cool kitchen tile, her chin resting on her favorite toy, a blue teddy bear, barely recognizable as such from all the chewing, tossing, and laundering it had endured. Her eyes had been following my every move, and the minute I picked up my keys she was on her feet, ready to go again, eager to be part of a new adventure. She clambered into the back of the old Ford Country Squire station wagon, circling herself a nest amidst the catch-pole, cat trap, pet carriers, gloves, old towels and blankets, packets of jerky treats and tins of sardines and tuna, all tools of the pet detective's trade.

Refreshed by the tea, I too was eager to be on my way. It seemed like a simple enough case. Money for old rope, one might say. A purebred show dog shouldn't be too hard to find. Somebody must recall having seen him.

"The game's afoot, Watson old girl! Let's go see how the show folk live," I said as I started the motor. It was always a bit of a cliff-hanger, but after a couple of protests the wagon coughed into life, and we were off.

♣ 2 ♣

Delilah Finds More
Than She's Looking For

WATSON IS A dog with an attitude. Perfectly well behaved when things are going her way, she can be downright stubborn if she thinks she is not being accorded her rightful place in the scheme of things. From the day I adopted her from the animal shelter, she had let me know that this was to be an equal partnership. She considers it her right, as well as her duty, to accompany me on all excursions. We are a team, and I leave her behind at my peril. Retribution is swift and remorseless, as I discovered to my cost the time I left her at home on one of our rare rainy days. In my absence she ripped up a couple of square yards of fitted carpeting. We didn't do that again. I'm a fast learner.

"We're in for a sticky drive," I told her as we headed inland. "You should have stayed home."

Taking that as an invitation to sit beside me, Watson clawed her way clumsily into the front seat, her heavy nails scraping the upholstery as she did so. "Hold on," I said, trying to forestall her. "I didn't mean . . ." But it's almost impossible to stop Watson in midcourse, especially when I'm driving. "Oh, all right." I gave up and concentrated on the drive.

Through some lapse in planning in the early sixties, Caltrans had given no thought to the eventual need for a free-way inland from the beach. While this had the advantage of isolating the beach community to some extent, that same isolation necessitated a long slow drive on surface streets to reach the county business center, or cultural and sports amenities. But having once reached the freeway, it took only a few minutes to the exit for Orange Blossom Heights, a semirural area on the outskirts of town.

Following Mrs. Lomax's directions I found myself driving by expensive ranch-style homes on large acreage, many with horse paddocks. Her house was at the end of a cul-de-sac, well set back from the street. A graceful stand of eucalyptus trees marked the rear of the property, which backed onto a flood control channel, while each side was bordered by dense shrubbery, including well-established thickets of privet and brilliant red and orange bougainvillaea, offering valuable seclusion and sound insulation for someone in the business of raising large noisy dogs.

I parked on the street in the shade of the huge, expertly pruned coral tree which dominated the front lawn. Checking my image in the rearview mirror, I pulled a comb through my unruly, mostly dark-brown curls, then rolled down the windows for Watson. She would not jump out unless I called, and no one was likely to attempt stealing her. Her fierce looks belied her sweet nature, and had saved me on more than one occasion.

A large, perhaps twenty-eight foot long, Winnebago motor home occupied most of the driveway. A head portrait of a German shepherd adorned the spare wheel cover attached to the rear of the cream-coloured vehicle, along with the words "Orange Blossom Kennels," etched in green to match the trim. The outer door of the motor home was open. Glancing in through the screen door as I passed, I noticed several large metal dog crates stacked inside. Obviously Jessica Lomax, like many breeders, used her recreational vehicle as a home away from home while on the show circuit, which would enable her to stay close to the show site, and to keep her dogs with her.

I hurried up the gravel walkway when I saw that my new client was waiting with ill-disguised impatience at the front door of the house. A pair of fine-looking German shepherds stood obediently by, observing my approach with dark, appraising eyes.

My preconceived notions of Jessica Lomax turned out to be mostly wrong. Far from the small, sharp-featured intellectual I had imagined, she presented a formidable figure. Heavyset for her height of approximately six feet, possibly as much as 180 pounds, she would make two of me. I had been right about the age, though, probably early fifties. Her astonishingly bright red hair, of a shade that nature had never devised, was arranged in short, tightly permed curls which allowed a pinkish-white scalp to show through. Her best features, large green eyes and creamy pale complexion, suggested that she had been a natural redhead in her youth. Theatrical was the way I would describe her attire. A low-necked, long-sleeved, frilly green blouse topped an ankle-length, full, multicoloured skirt. Giant silver and enamel German shepherd earrings, fashioned so that the body, legs, and tail moved independently of the head forming the button ear-piece, were matched by an enormous pendant adorning her ample bosom. Jessica Lomax would cut quite an imposing figure in the show ring, I imagined.

She peered at me disapprovingly through pink-tinted glasses. "Mrs. Doolittle," she greeted. "You sounded younger over the phone." Her overbearing manner made her appear even larger.

I was used to this reaction.

"Don't let the grey streaks fool you," I said. (Maybe Evie's right, I thought, as I handed Mrs. Lomax my business card, perhaps I should get a tint.) Aloud I said, "Lots of experience. Never met an animal I couldn't handle." I reached down and petted the dogs.

"These are Herbie's offspring," she said proudly. "This

is Sheba. She's the only breeding bitch I have right now. Major will finish next month," she continued, referring to the show circuit point system. Bending down, she demonstrated Major's stance for my admiration—stacking, I believe they call it—setting his legs just so, putting her hand gently under his chin to show off his cleanly chiseled head. Major, obviously used to such goings-on, submitted with patience.

Letting him go with a "good dog," she pulled a couple of freeze-dried liver treats from her skirt pocket for him and for Sheba.

"Herbie's sperm has been sent to breeders in Australia and Europe." Delighted to have an audience, she made no attempt to hide her pride. "They say their best dogs have come from Herbie."

I nodded with bemused approval. Artificial insemination for canines or, for that matter, any other species, was not something I was up on, but I gathered from her tone that Herbie was a champ in that arena also.

"Why didn't you take the dogs with you to San Diego?" I asked, recalling the crates I had observed in the Winnebago.

"I wasn't showing, and I didn't want to be distracted from my judging duties," she said with an air that indicated she felt she had been obliged to state the obvious.

My new client showed me into a large comfortable drawing room, the walls of which were covered with photographs of German shepherds, and of Mrs. Lomax receiving and Mrs. Lomax presenting trophies. A glass-fronted oak cabinet held crystal bowls and vases, a silver plate coffee service and, in the centre, a large silver loving cup.

On the mantelpiece over the grey stone fireplace stood a carved wooden box, which one might guess contained somebody's ashes. A small picture of a German shepherd was inserted in the lid. Mrs. Lomax followed my gaze. "That's the founder of my line," she said, her eyes misting. "He passed away some years back." What a pity, I thought. And now Herbie's disappeared. Well, not for long. I'll find him.

"This is Herbie." Jessica handed me a 5×7 duplicate of the coloured studio portrait that hung over the fireplace. A beautiful creature, the keen, intelligent, and composed expression conveying an unmistakable look of quality and nobility, Herbie was a more mature edition of Major and Sheba. Though to be quite honest, not being an expert on the breed, all the Lomax dogs looked pretty much alike to me.

"Mrs. Lomax . . ." I began.

"Call me Jessica," she ordered. I was to learn that she always ordered, or demanded, never requested. It must come from years of training, and expecting obedience from, rather large, strong-willed dogs. I doubted anyone, man or beast, ever got the better of Jessica Lomax. Well, it would take more than liver treats to put anything over on me. I hoped she wasn't going to try to tell me how to do my job.

I tucked the photograph in my bag and began again.

"You're quite sure he's nowhere on the premises, or in the neighbourhood?"

"Quite sure. I've done a thorough search of the area, and even asked the people next door if they've seen him." By her expression it was clear that speaking to the neighbours was something she would do only with the utmost reluctance.

"I must ask you to get onto this right away, Mrs. Doolittle," she continued, "because if anyone picks him up I'll never get him back."

"May I take a look around?" I had it in mind that the dog might possibly have been taken ill. He could have got into some poison, possibly antifreeze or snailbait, gone into convulsions, and be lying sick somewhere, maybe even dead.

A tour of the house revealed little other than to confirm Jessica's status as a first-class dog breeder and judge. Framed pictures and certificates, some with purple and gold, or red, white, and blue ribbon rosettes attached to them, adorned the walls of the hallway leading to the kitchen.

Only in the case of the cats, it seemed, was Jessica's taste less refined. Two elderly and definitely unpedigreed tabbies, who had been dozing on a pile of clothes in a laundry basket, yawned at my approach, looking none the worse for their recent neglect. Jessica, obviously a meticulous housekeeper, had done a quick job of cleaning up the kitty litter. The kitchen was spotless, and only the faintest trace of litter box odour lingered as a reminder of the pet sitter's negligence.

"Your house is beautiful," I remarked. "It must take a lot of work to keep it up. Do you have help?"

"A cleaning woman comes in once a week. Tuesday mornings. I've already called her," said Jessica, anticipating my next question. "Herbie was still here when she came last Tuesday."

The fastidious housekeeping extended even to the outer buildings. A kitchen door led into the tidiest garage I had ever seen. It housed a dark blue, late model Chrysler Imperial, little else. If there was any clutter here, it was concealed inside neatly arranged cabinets.

A large doggie door had been set into the opposite wall, giving access to the recently hosed down cement dog enclosure, which ran the length of the garage.

We exited the garage through a side door and crossed the yard to a large horse barn, which offered possibilities as a hideout for a sick or injured dog. But on closer inspection it appeared not to have seen any signs of life, canine or equine, for quite a while. No Herbie here.

I looked around the grounds beyond the immediate outbuildings. On the far side of the otherwise empty paddock stood a large redwood doghouse, the sloping roof weatherproofed with heavyweight plastic sheeting. From this angle, with the entrance facing away from the house, I was unable to see if it contained a dog, though it would have

to be an extremely lethargic or ailing animal not to have
been alerted by my approach.

"Oh, no," said Jessica, anticipating my objective. "Herbie never uses the doghouse. Don't know why I haven't
got rid of it before now. My dogs always sleep indoors
unless I'm away. Then they're confined to the dog run.
Anyway, if he'd been in there he would have come when
I called."

Her voice trailing behind me, I made my way through
the gate and across the paddock, Sheba and Major romping
ahead. Reaching the doghouse they stopped, sniffed around,
and started to whimper, alerting me to trouble even before
the stomach-wrenching odour reached my nostrils. I braced
myself. This was not going to be pleasant.

Cautiously I raised the burlap flap tacked across the entrance, disturbing a cloud of flies as I did so. Was my assignment to be over before it had fairly begun?

I was right. Definitely dead. But definitely not Herbie.

I'm not one to scream, but I admit I've never been closer
to it. The sound that emerged from my throat was more of
a shuddering gasp.

❖ 3 ❖

Delilah Meets the Law

HURRIEDLY DROPPING THE flap, I took an involuntary step backward, almost falling over Jessica, who had come up behind me.

"What is it?" she said, seeing my dismay.

Commanding the dogs to a sit/stay, I again lifted the flap, revealing the body of a young man. At least, I judged him to be young by the slender build clothed in tee shirt and jeans. The grotesque face indicated only that its owner had come to a violent and unnatural end. The doghouse barely accommodated the body, which appeared to be folded in a fetal position, the feet poking out just beyond the entrance.

Jessica leaned forward, took a quick look at the body, then stood back, gaping at the grisly scene in silence.

"Do you know who this is?" I asked her. She shook her head vacantly. Horrified as we both were, still I was surprised by her seeming inability to come to grips with the situation. I had known her barely an hour, yet I would have judged her to be capable of rising to any occasion.

I waited for her to do something. It was her doghouse, after all. But after a few seconds during which it seemed that she was incapable of taking any initiative, I gave her a gentle shove. "Go call 911," I said. "And take the dogs with you. The police won't want them underfoot."

At the mention of the police Jessica's creamy skin turned ashen, as she finally appeared to grasp the enormity of what had happened. Still she hesitated. "But you . . ."

"I'll stay here," I said. Without a word, she turned and hurried back to the house, the dogs at her heels.

For some reason it seemed wrong to leave the body alone, though why I felt compelled to stay, I don't know. The poor soul had obviously been here alone for several days already. Clearly he could come to no further harm. But as his finder I did feel a certain obligation.

I looked around at the peaceful scene made monstrous by my discovery. The paddock, shielded from the neighbours by the dense shrubbery, was in need of mowing, and the sweet smell of the tall grass mingled wretchedly with the odour of decaying flesh in the warm summer sun. The only sounds were the faint hum of distant traffic and the chirping of birds awakened from their siesta by the cooling of the late afternoon breeze, quite oblivious to the gruesome scene before them. Flies buzzing around my face brought me back from my woolgathering with a start, and I realized I was still holding on to the tip of the burlap flap.

Waving the flies away from the dead man's face, I noticed what appeared to be a heavy dog collar around his neck. It was not the usual type of collar, but an electronic device, the kind some dog trainers use, fitted with a small boxlike receiver. Could he possibly have died from some kind of shock? Surely not. Such collars, though I detested them and felt they were used only by trainers too lazy or inept to train dogs by traditional methods, were guaranteed not to harm the animal, just to get its attention.

I dismissed any notion of a bizarre accident. This could only be foul play. I looked around the paddock with renewed interest, and for the first time noticed that the grass from the gate to the doghouse was smoothed down as if something heavy, possibly the body, had been dragged across it.

All conjecture was put aside by the sound of approaching police sirens, and soon Jessica was hurrying back across the paddock with two uniformed policemen in tow, her composure somewhat restored.

I have this ability, due in part to my size, I'm sure, but perhaps also due to my inborn English reserve, that enables me to fade unnoticed into the background. Whether it's a gift or a curse depends on the circumstances, but I have a theory (not one that I'm likely to put to the test) that I could run starkers the length of our Surf City pier and not a head would turn. At times this seeming invisibility is infuriating, as when I'm the last to be waited on in a store, but it does have its uses. Like now. Jessica had been asked to go back to the house, but I stood there, ignored, apparently unnoticed, quietly observing the goings-on, eavesdropping, if you will, while the police went about their business.

"What's that around his neck?" asked one of the officers, a tall thin young man who looked like he could never get enough to eat.

"Beats me," replied his partner, obviously some years the other's senior. By contrast he looked like he'd put away too many good dinners.

"It's an electronic dog collar," I offered. Both men turned and regarded me seriously, as if seeing me for the first time.

"Do you live here?" the senior of the two asked. As he turned toward me I could see his nameplate. B. Offley, it read.

"No." I handed him my card. "At the request of Mrs. Lomax I'm investigating the disappearance—" As soon as the words were out of my mouth I knew they were not well chosen.

"Investigating, eh!" Offley thrust his jowly face closer to mine. "Just what are you investigating?"

I started again, explaining my business, that I was a pet detective. Again, wrong choice of words.

"A what detective?"

"A pet detective. I help people find their missing—"

"A *pet* detective? What's that, some kind of mascot?" said Offley, guffawing at his wit and nudging his fellow officer to make sure he got the joke.

Turning to me, the younger man, whose nameplate announced J. Perkins, looked a little embarrassed by his companion's oafishness. "The detective will get your statement later," he said apologetically. "You can tell him about the collar. Meanwhile, please wait in the house."

They hustled me back to the house, where I was obliged to wait in the kitchen with Jessica until the detective arrived.

Poor Jessica, obviously shaken by the macabre goings-on at her home during her absence, was not the best of company. I tried talking to her about our discovery, to speculate on who the victim might be and how he came to be in her doghouse, but she seemed totally distracted, quite incapable of holding a decent conversation. Hardly surprising in the circumstances, I empathized. Unable to settle down, she fidgeted about the kitchen, first wiping down countertops, then aimlessly glancing through magazines stacked neatly on a wickerwork étagère, then picking up a dish towel to dab away invisible spots from the unblemished refrigerator door.

I changed the subject to San Diego, scene of the recent dog show. I mentioned I had close friends there, then, recalling a breeder acquaintance, said, "I wonder if you know a friend of mine, Molly Rhys-Davies? She's a Corgi breeder. It's quite likely that she was at the show you attended."

"Yes, I know Molly." Jessica's attention revived briefly at the mention of the subject closest to her heart. "She did quite well. Her Pembroke bitch took best of breed but didn't show well in group. Needs to . . ." But it was an effort, and her attention wandered again. She was too agitated to concentrate on anything for more than a few minutes at a time.

I sat down at the kitchen table, and immediately one of the tabbies jumped into my lap and began kneading to make herself comfortable. Her claws bit into my legs through my cotton slacks and I stood up again, intent on returning her to the laundry basket. As I did so, I caught sight of a photograph of what appeared to be this same cat, on the top shelf of the étagère. Attached to the frame was a purple ribbon rosette bearing the legend "California Cat Show, Best Household Pet," and dated several years earlier. So, even the lowly moggies had to prove themselves. It seemed Jessica needed to excel in everything she did.

"You show your cats, too?" I said in yet another futile attempt at conversation.

"What? Oh, yes. The cats," was all she managed. I gave up any further attempt to engage her in conversation, and Jessica turned her attention to scouring a spotless sink.

I was getting hungry. I wondered if Jessica might offer me something to eat, but the strange turn of events seemed to have robbed her of all awareness of the amenities due a guest.

I looked around for something to read. Not feeling at liberty to go wandering around the house uninvited, however, I was limited to what I could find in the kitchen. I turned to the pile of magazines Jessica had been fidgeting with earlier: *Dog World, Southern California Dog*, the *AKC Gazette*, a studbook register, some kind of bus or railway timetable, a pet supply catalog. I glanced through the catalog for a few minutes but soon lost interest. Watson had all the toys, dishes, collars, and shampoos she needed. Certainly she wouldn't be caught dead in the cute red raincoat and booties modelled by a Rottweiler who looked ready to die from embarrassment himself.

Watson. Oh, dear, she was still in the car. She must need a potty break by now. I reached the front door just as Officer Offley came in, accompanied by another man in civilian clothes. This must be the detective in charge.

"Hold on, where do you think you're going?" said Offley.

"Just going to let my dog out of the car."

"That can wait. Detective Mallory here has some questions for you."

Detective Jack Mallory, Homicide Division, Surf City Police Department, was a surprise. Not at all what I had expected. But then I hardly knew what to expect. My knowledge of American policemen had heretofore been formed solely by the cinema and television. But here was no stolid "Just the facts, ma'am" Sgt. Friday. Nor an improbably handsome *Miami Vice* hero, nor yet a scruffy *NYPD Blue* type. Detective Mallory didn't fit any stereotypical profile I might have had in mind.

Detective Jack Mallory was, well, nice. Not tall, not short, a little on the heavy side, but comfortable. Mid to late fifties. His thick greying hair longer than I would have considered regulation, curling at the tips of his ears. Bushy eyebrows over intelligent blue-grey eyes. His tan didn't come from any athletic activity, I guessed, but he must spend a lot of time outdoors. His outfit of dark blue blazer, grey slacks, eggshell-blue shirt, and tie in a discreet plaid of blue and grey, though not obviously expensive, were of a better cut and quality than one might have expected. At another time and place I might have checked for a wedding ring. All this I observed while he was talking to Jessica.

"Mrs. Lomax, I'm afraid we're going to have to break up the doghouse in order to remove the victim," he was saying. As if the poor woman would ever want to see that doomed edifice again, much less use it. She shrugged helplessly.

She was asked to wait in the living room while he interviewed me. I was relieved I got to go first. I was anxious to get out of there.

Detective Mallory shook my hand, and politely but very astutely took me through the events leading up to my discovery of the body, beginning with the phone call from Jessica.

He had the ability to quickly put a person at ease. But though my experience of policemen was limited, I had been around long enough to recognize an old smoothie when I met one. I knew instinctively that his low-key demeanour was calculated to lead people, guilty or not, into saying more than they intended.

"I understand you're a"—he glanced at my card—"a pet detective?" He seemed more than a little amused at my reason for being at the scene. For my part, I suddenly found my card, with its logo of a Watsonlike dog in a deerstalker hat, acutely embarrassing. Until that moment, I had thought it rather clever.

"That's right," I replied with all the dignity I could muster. "I help people find their lost pets."

"Much call for that kind of thing, is there?" he asked. He looked down at his notebook as if to hide a grin, but gave no further indication that he regarded my profession as anything but slightly unusual.

"You'd be surprised," I replied. "It's amazing how careless people can be with their precious pets." I hoped Jessica was out of earshot.

"And that is the sole purpose of your visit here today?" he asked.

"Of course," I replied. "I didn't make the acquaintance of Mrs. Lomax until a few hours ago." I was glad I had nothing to hide from that sharp gaze.

"Have you ever met the victim before?" was his next question.

"Most certainly not," I replied. "I told you, I'm here for purely business reasons. I barely know Mrs. Lomax, much less the unfortunate occupant of her doghouse."

"You're English, aren't you?" he asked. Well, at least he got that right.

"Yes, I am," I said. Was he going to ask me about my

immigration status? This interview was making me extremely uncomfortable. But . . .

"My family is from Britain originally," was all he said.

"Really," I replied, as graciously as possible. I suppose I should have gone on to ask him from what part, but I was in no mood for small talk right now. Watson was waiting.

"Look here," I went on. "Will this take much longer? I've got to see to my dog. I left her in the car." Though Watson was very good, I felt that we were getting close to the limits of her endurance.

"Just a few more questions, Mrs. Doolittle. Almost done." Detective Mallory consulted his notebook again. "I understand you can identify the dog collar around the victim's neck," he said.

He was making me feel guilty again. "That particular collar?" I asked, wondering if he was trying to trap me. "No. I'm not too familiar with such things, but it looks to me like the type of collar that's used for obedience work and field training."

"Field training?"

"Yes. Training sporting dogs to retrieve."

"How does it work?"

"I've never used one. But I understand that the trainer uses a remote control device to give the dog a shock to correct behaviour."

The interview ended with his request that I stop by the station the following day to sign my statement.

By the time I left, several more vehicles and officials had arrived, and the neighbours were out in force. A white van bearing the words CRIME SCENE painted on the side in what seemed to me to be unnecessarily large letters left one in no doubt that "something was up." As I ducked under the yellow tape securing the area, one of the neighbours fixed me with a piercing stare. All had been sweetness and light in the quiet cul-de-sac until I came on the scene, setting off a sequence of events to disturb the tranquility of their high-priced neighbourhood. I waited until we had turned the corner before letting Watson out to go to the loo.

I was glad to get away. Though I felt bad about leaving Jessica at such a time, as she talked to the police she had appeared to be regaining control of herself. Before I left she had signed my contract, and on handing me the cheque for the deposit had reminded me again how anxious she was that I get on with the search for Herbie.

There was not much I could do about that today. It was past six o'clock and the shelters were already closed. I would go on my rounds tomorrow, after I had interviewed the pet sitter.

I headed for home. By the time I drove along Pacific Coast Highway and turned inland the half block to my tiny beach bungalow, the sun was no more than an orange glow behind the pier.

I fed Watson, then, reaching for the Beefeater's, a present from Evie the last time she came through the duty-free shop at Heathrow, fixed myself the long-delayed gin and tonic. It would sharpen my appetite for the tin of tomato soup and Marmite sandwich, all I had the energy to fix that evening. On the way home I had stopped off at a drive-through for a hamburger, but the recurring vision of the decaying body in the doghouse was playing havoc with my digestive system, and I ended up giving the hamburger to Watson, who has the digestion of a garbage disposal.

While the soup warmed I played back my messages.

My ad in the lost and found columns attracted an intriguing variety of animal-related calls, as if a certain talent for locating lost pets presumed a fountain of knowledge on all kinds of animal behaviour and care. I was glad to help when I could, and the contacts could be good for business.

Beep. A man's voice: *"Please call me back as soon as possible and tell me what I should do with this skunk I've trapped."*

"Why didn't he call before he trapped the poor thing?" I asked of Watson. "It's probably too late to help either one of them now."

Beep. A woman this time: *"Is there anything we can do about people who smoke in pet shops? It can't be good for the animals to have to breathe secondhand smoke all day long."*

"She's got a point there, Watson, but it's not a cause we have time to champion right now. We have Herbie to find."

Beep. An older man's voice: *"What can I do to stop the neighbour's cat from hanging around my bird feeder?"* Not much. It's the circle of life, luv.

Beep. Evie again. She was getting cross. "Yes, yes," I murmured. You're the very next on my list. Her voice droned on, and I felt my eyelids drooping, but the next call brought me awake with a start.

· 4 ·

Friends in Need

" 'ALLO, MRS. D. It's me, Tony."

No need to tell me, I'd recognize that Cockney accent anywhere! *"I'm in a bit of bovver,"* he said. *"Do me a favour and go to the shelter and do the necessary for Trixie."*

Tiptoe Tony was a familiar figure in our beach community. An avid surfer despite his advancing years, some said he had come by his monicker from the way that, short and wiry, bandy-legged, surfboard under his arm, he scampered across the hot sand looking like some kind of demented sea-elf. Others, referring to his occasional brushes with the law, hinted at a more sinister reason for the nickname. But all acknowledged his surfing skills. He was a former senior men's surfing champion, and still hit the waves regularly. Other than that, and the fact that he lived in a nearby trailer park, I didn't know much about him. His fondness for animals, and the fact that he had been an acquaintance of my late husband, whose own business pursuits had occasionally been called into question, were really his only claims on my friendship.

Probably the "bovver," or bother, Tony found himself in was the local jail, and Trixie, his Jack Russell terrier who accompanied him everywhere, would have been incarcerated in the animal shelter next door. In emergencies, such as when a person is arrested or taken to hospital, their pets are impounded at the shelter until other arrangements can be made for their care. "Doing the necessary" for Trixie meant bailing her out. It wasn't the first time Tony had called on my help, but I could hardly refuse. I didn't like to think of the little dog languishing in the shelter for any longer than need be. I'd be there tomorrow looking for Herbie, anyway, so it would be no inconvenience.

I finished my soup and sandwich, and, thus fortified, returned Evie's calls.

"Finally," she said peevishly. "Where *have* you been?" Without giving me a chance to reply, she went on to explain that she was coming to nearby Newport Beach the following day to collect a new car. Coming by train and driving back. I was to pick her up at the railway station and take her to the car dealership. Of course. It was time for her biannual pilgrimage to Mercedes Mecca. I had a vague recollection that she had mentioned this to me the last time we had spoken.

"I've made late lunch reservations at the Mountain View Lodge. I know you like it there. My treat," she added, trying to soften what she might know would be an inconvenience at the last minute. She refrained from mentioning that the Lodge's outdoor dining area would allow her to smoke her endless ciggies.

It was a nice idea, one I would have responded to with pleasure if I hadn't already had other plans, which now included not only looking for Herbie, but a visit to the police station to sign my statement, and springing Trixie from doggie jail.

But there was little point in explaining to Evie that I had work to do. She had always refused to take my job seriously. Her plans were made, the hour was late, and after all, if I had called her back sooner she could have made other arrangements. So summoning what grace I had left at the end of an exceedingly tiring day, I agreed to meet her.

"It will do you good to get out," she went on. "I don't know what you do with yourself all day in that dreary shack of a place."

"I prefer to think of it as rustic," I replied, trying not to feel unjustly injured by this cutting remark. I knew her well enough to know that she only wanted the best for me.

"You can call it rustic if you like. I call it downright shabby, and I will never understand why Roger didn't leave you better provided for." She was skating on thin ice here, referring to my dear departed, who for all his faults had been utterly devoted to me, and well she knew it. But indeed she was right. The house was all Roger had left me, and even that is heavily mortgaged.

"Something's got to be done," Evie went on hastily. "I've met this really nice man. He'd be ideal for you. We'll talk about it tomorrow."

I tried to tell her I was perfectly capable of finding my own RNM if I felt in need of one. But Evie, ever headstrong and thoughtless of other people's feelings, rattled on regardless about what was good for me, until finally she said, "Well, you mustn't keep me chatting any longer. Howard has just come in from his meeting, he'll be wanting his drinkie. See you tomorrow."

I switched on the television, but there was no mention of my grim discovery at the Lomax place in the nightly litany of murder, mayhem, and madness that passes for news these days. I guessed events had unfolded too late to make the early evening report. It would probably be on *News at Eleven*, but I'd be fast asleep by then.

Enough of endless chat. I needed some peace and quiet. I hit the off switch on the remote and took a refill of my g & t out onto the patio where I relaxed on the chaise lounge, listening to the surf and contemplating the extraordinary events of the day. The full moon illuminated the backyard as if it were daylight, creating sharp shadows among the hibiscus, the potted plants, the stone birdbath that I needed to remember to refill tomorrow morning. The scent of night-blooming jasmine and honeysuckle was almost over-powering, but intermingled with the floral perfume I could detect faint traces of salt air wafting on the prevailing westerly breeze over the Pacific Ocean a few yards away.

"This is the life," I said to Watson, as she settled at my feet, "I don't care what Evie says."

♣ 5 ♣

Delilah Hits the Road

As SOON AS the commuter traffic eased the next morning I headed out to see Jim Ratchett, owner of the pet-sitting service Jessica had hired. The name sounded familiar, but I couldn't connect it with any of the pet sitters of my acquaintance.

I needed to find out when Ratchett had last visited Jessica's house. By now he must have learned of Herbie's disappearance, if he hadn't already known. It was possible that the German shepherd had proved to be more difficult to handle than either he or Jessica had anticipated, and after the dog had run off, the pet sitter had panicked and abandoned his post. Though from what Jessica had told me, that scenario wasn't very likely. She had hired Ratchett specifically because of his dog handling abilities.

I wondered if the police had questioned him yet. The morning's *Los Angeles Times* had offered only the briefest report of the crime. "Body Found Stuffed in Doghouse" appeared on page ten of the local news section. The victim had not been identified, the report saying only that the young man's name was being withheld pending notification of the family. It was not known how long he had been dead. An autopsy was scheduled for this morning, the report concluded. There had been no mention of the training collar.

Despite the early hour the drive inland was hot and sticky. It didn't help that the air conditioner was on the blink. Rolling down the windows only invited in a nauseating cocktail of dust and car exhaust. Watson roused at the sound of my muttered curses on all things automotive.

"Never mind, old girl," I told her. "When we win the lottery we'll get it fixed." I pondered this for a moment, then continued. "Who am I kidding! When we win the lottery we're going to trade in this old bucket of bolts for a Land Rover, like Queen Elizabeth's." Only then would I be willing to subscribe to the California myth that you are what you drive.

Even my bargain-basement safari-type outfit wasn't helping. That's what Evie calls it, anyway. She says it's boring. Boring, maybe, but I happen to like khaki, olive, and tan earth tones, and find cotton the most comfortable for this climate. At least by keeping to the same basic colours I don't waste time trying to decide what goes with what every morning. It's not Banana Republic, but it's very practical. My one extravagance are the desert boots I treated myself to the last time I was in England. With good shoes on one's feet one is prepared for anything. It's a Brit thing. All that standing around in damp weather instills in one at a very early age the importance of being well shod. Show me an irritable person and I'll show you someone whose feet hurt.

Earlier that morning I had stopped by the twenty-four-hour print shop and run off flyers describing Herbie and offering a reward for his return. LOST: GERMAN SHEPHERD, MALE, NO COLLAR, BLACK & TAN, VICINITY ORANGE BLOSSOM HEIGHTS. REWARD, and my telephone number. I used a stock photo from my dog breed file to illustrate the flyer, which I planned to distribute in Jessica's neighbourhood on my way back from Jim Ratchett's. His place was off the next freeway exit past Jessica's.

Distributing flyers is a time-consuming but necessary

part of the pet detective's job. The wider the radius covered, the better the chances of retrieving the pet. I also place ads in the lost and found classified sections of the local newspapers, check the shelters, repeatedly, talk to neighbours and delivery people, inquire at local pet shops and animal hospitals, and check the parks and school yards. Children can be especially helpful. They know where every pet in the neighbourhood resides, and are always sure to spot a strange dog in the area.

"My dear Watson," I said to my partner dozing alongside me. "Let's think about this. For a well-trained dog to disappear like that, he was either scared by something, he decided to go looking for Jessica, or somebody stole him." Watson opened her eyes and appeared to think this over for a moment, then gave me a look as if to say, "Don't ask me to explain the actions of an overbred show dog," and went back to sleep.

According to Jessica, Herbie had never run away before, even when she had left him at home alone. So that left being scared off or stolen, and the more I thought about it the more I was convinced that, either way, the dog's disappearance had something to do with the murder.

But I should not so quickly dismiss the possibility that he had simply run away. One should never overlook the obvious. While people will often claim that their pet has been stolen, in fact it's far more likely that it has run off, either when at long last it has the opportunity to do so, such as when a gate has been inadvertently left open, or because it has been frightened into it, by something like a thunderstorm or fireworks. Or a murder. I was back to that again.

What about theft?

"Who would steal a dog like that?" I asked Watson. No matter how good his looks, a champion dog is only as good as his written pedigree. Without papers he's just another dog, with no real value for stud or show. Besides, it was the cute, fluffy numbers (the poodles, the Shih Tzus, the

Maltese), so easy to just pick up, that were more likely to be stolen and sold, or perhaps ransomed. They might even be kept by well-meaning finders, reluctant to turn them in to the shelter. The larger and medium-sized mixed breed dogs were harder to catch, and more likely to be picked up by animal control and impounded. If they were not hit by a car first.

A glance through my DOA notes for dead animal pickup in Jessica's neighbourhood revealed only a couple of flat cats and an opossum. No German shepherds of any size, sex, or colour.

"So who might have stolen Herbie?" If Watson had an opinion, she was keeping it to herself, but it helped to air my theories aloud. "In the first place, it has to be someone who is not afraid to approach a large dog. If he is out to make a few dollars he'll watch the classifieds, then call and demand a reward when the 'Lost' ad appears. In that case, Watson, we'll be hearing from him before long." For this reason I always used my own telephone number on the flyers and in classified ads, rather than that of my client.

Then there were the sleazy characters who stole dogs to sell for laboratory research. But as far as I knew there were no bunchers operating in the area at the moment.

Reaching my exit, I followed a road running parallel to the freeway, and soon spotted the sign I was looking for. It was so badly in need of repainting I could barely make out the words: "JIM RATCHETT, DOG TRAINER, SPORT AND SENTRY," and in smaller letters underneath: "pet sitting, kennels, field work."

Turning from the dirt driveway into the small parking area, the first thing I clapped eyes on was a battered old truck with wooden side supports. Several metal cages were stacked in the truck bed. An offensive bumper sticker, fortunately barely legible through the dirt, adorned the dented rear bumper, while a half-naked hula doll dangled from the rearview mirror, her arms folded provocatively behind her head.

Now I knew why the name was familiar. I had seen this truck at the animal shelter on many occasions. My heart sank.

• 6 •

Delilah Meets an Old Foe

ONE OF JIM Ratchett's sidelines was renting out mean-looking dogs to protect used-car lots, junkyards, and the like. He was always on the lookout for cheap dogs for the business, and the source of many of these was the animal shelter. No Doberman or Rottweiler, however aged or decrepit, was euthanized on the days Ratchett came around. Some people, myself included, felt that euthanasia was a kinder fate for these animals than the brutal treatment they often underwent to be made suitably aggressive for guard dog duty.

It was only by luck and good timing that Watson hadn't ended up in Ratchett's hands. Her original owners had acquired her for breeding purposes, but when it became apparent that she was unable to produce a litter, they turned her in to the shelter. As luck would have it, I was at the shelter that day, and a few minutes was all it took to convince both of us that we were meant for each other.

That was the first time I ran into Ratchett. We had both been looking at Watson in the kennel at the same time, and if I'd had any hesitation about whether or not to adopt her, Ratchett's presence would have convinced me. We had turned toward the kennel office almost in unison, and I had to break into a trot to stay ahead of him. Rita, the office manager, who had told me about the dog when I first arrived, and who knew Ratchett all too well, had seen me coming and greeted me with, ''I have your paperwork on kennel fifty-nine all ready for you, Mrs. Doolittle. Here you go. She's all yours.'' I owe her one.

Now Watson and I were about to come face-to-face with Jim Ratchett again, and on his own turf this time.

With Watson walking calmly at my heels, the leash slack between us, we made our way over to the converted trailer which I guessed served as an office.

About fifty feet beyond the trailer was a chain-link and cement kennel structure, containing a dozen or so runs where the guard dogs were presumably kept when they were off duty. The remainder of the property consisted of a large field or meadow and what, from this distance, appeared to be a small pond. The field backed on to the same flood control channel that defined the rear boundary of Jessica's place.

It now occurred to me that Herbie might well have headed in this direction, running along the channel's adjacent bike path. In the pet detective business it helps if one can develop the ability to see things from an animal's viewpoint. A person leaving home normally uses the front door. An animal, on the other hand, leaves by the nearest means available, blundering instinctively out the gate, over the fence, through the hedge, prompted more by opportunity than conscious intent. Herbie could have gone in any direction, including this one. And Ratchett might already have found him. I kept my eyes peeled.

No one responded to my knock on the office door, and I was about to check out the dog runs in back when I heard a sharp whistle and a distant bark. Turning my gaze back to the field, I saw that Ratchett had now come into view. He was working with a pair of Brittany spaniels who were splashing about at the edge of the pond, their orange and

white coats vivid against the surrounding parched brown
turf.

Training dogs for hunting was another of Ratchett's sidelines. From this distance it was difficult to tell precisely
what they were doing. It looked like some kind of retrieving
exercise. As I might have guessed, Ratchett was using electronic training collars. One of the dogs appeared to be responding quite well. The other just didn't seem to be able
to get the hang of what was required of her, and each time
she failed to respond in the correct manner she would get
a jolt from the transmitter. The resulting yelp was heart-
breaking.

I'd seen enough. Reminding myself of my mission, I
took a deep breath and made up my mind to try to be
pleasant. The man had information I needed. I made my
way across the field, Watson keeping pace with my determined stride. I waited until I was within hearing distance,
then spoke. "Excuse me, Mr. Ratchett?"

He turned. "Yes," he said curtly. His scowl indicated
he was not at all pleased to have his training methods observed. The time that had passed since our last encounter
had done nothing to improve his disposition, it seemed. He
still wore the same guarded expression of one permanently
at odds with the world. Though only of medium height and
whippet-thin, there was an air of menace about him. His
bullying treatment of the helpless animals under his control
was his way of compensating for his own shortcomings, I
decided.

"Might I have a word?"

"What about?" Jim Ratchett was a man of few words,
even fewer of them pleasant. "Wanna sell the dog?" I
tightened my grip on Watson's leash and forced a smile. I
wondered if he recognized me.

"No," I said. "My name's Delilah Doolittle. I help people find their lost pets." I handed him my card. "I believe
you were pet-sitting for Mrs. Lomax while she was away
last week?"

"Well, I was planning to do it myself, but I got busy so my nephew Steve took care of it."

So he'd sent somebody else. Jessica had expected Ratchett to do the job personally. That might explain why Herbie had been allowed to escape.

"Well, unfortunately, her prize shepherd Herbie has disappeared, and she has hired me to help find him."

"Well, well. So Herbert Fitzherbert ran off, did he?" he chuckled. A dry, humourless sound. "Bet she's pretty sick about that."

The thought of Jessica's distress appeared to amuse him, despite the fact that his company could be held responsible. That thought must have suddenly occurred to him. Adjusting his dirty white baseball cap, he said, "Listen. That dog's a mean s.o.b. Jessica's the only one can handle him. I told her he might be a problem. So if she's trying to pin this on me . . ." He broke off, shrugged, spat on the ground. I disliked him more by the minute.

"All she's interested in is getting the dog back," I said. "I don't think she's going to blame anyone under the circumstances."

"What circumstances?" He looked wary.

I was going to tell him about the body in the doghouse, but thought better of it when it occurred to me that if, as I was beginning to suspect, the body was that of the pet sitter—his nephew, as it now turned out—I'd better leave the telling to the authorities.

"Oh, well, you know, she blames herself, and feels guilty that she went away and left him," I prevaricated. That wasn't too far from the truth. "If you could give me your nephew's address or phone number, I'd like to ask him when he last saw the dog. No intention of placing blame, you understand. We just want to get the dog back."

"Well, I tell you, I don't believe it. But I don't want no trouble. Better see what we can do to find the dog, I guess. Don't know Stevie's number offhand, he keeps moving around. Come to think of it, I haven't seen or heard from him since he took on the Lomax job. Think he's staying with his sister Debbie over in Westgrove right now. She'll know where he is, anyhow. Come over to the office and I'll give you her number.''

While he was occupied with penning the spaniels, who, grateful for a break, flopped in the shade on the cool cement run, their leg feathers muddied from the workout in the pond, I cast a quick look around the kennel for Herbie. I didn't trust this man, and was quite prepared for him to try to lie his way out of it if I did spot the dog. But there was no sign of my quarry in the sad-looking assortment of large crossbreeds and purebred discards. What a wretched way for them to end their days.

Perhaps sensing my disgust with his operation, Ratchett was silent as he accompanied me back to the office. Thumbing through the pages of a dog-eared notebook, he found his niece's telephone number, which I jotted on the back of one of my cards. Then, with a curt nod, he turned back to his interrupted task, transmitter in hand. Casting a last pitying look in the direction of the hapless Brittanys, I headed back to my car.

I was about to pull out of the parking lot when a police car arrived, with Detective Mallory in the passenger seat. He waved me down and approached, resting his arm on my car's open window. Watson growled. She doesn't like people putting their heads, hands, or anything else inside our car.

"Quiet," I murmured. "Let's not annoy the nice policeman.''

"Well, Mrs. Doolittle," Mallory was saying. "What are you doing here so early in the morning?''

"I explained yesterday. Mrs. Lomax has hired me to find her dog, so I thought I would start by asking the pet sitter when he last saw him.''

"You're just here looking for the dog, then. No other reason?'' He obviously had doubts.

"No. What other reason could there possibly be?" I replied.

"You tell me," he said.

"I don't know what you're implying, Detective, but I can assure you that—"

He interrupted me. "I'm implying that you might be trying to do a little amateur detective work yourself. And I'm not *implying*," (he laid heavy emphasis on the word) "I'm telling you, you can get into a lot of trouble if you take this pet detective business too far." His casual low-key manner was strangely at odds with the directness of his remarks.

As he finished speaking he turned his attention to a hawk circling in the thermals high overhead.

"Red-tailed," I offered.

"No, it's a red-shouldered. Tail's longer," he replied. He was probably right. He spoke with an authority that brooked no argument, and Detective Mallory was not the kind of man, I felt, to make such a statement unless he was quite sure of himself. So, he was a birder. That would explain the tan and the searching eyes. A kindred spirit. Too bad we were getting off to such a bad start. I might have asked him if he'd been lucky enough to catch sight of the rare Sooty Tern which had been present in our local wetlands since midsummer. It would be a treasured addition to any birder's life list. But Detective Mallory's body language indicated "strictly business."

I sighed. Wasn't there a point in both our investigations where we might assist each other? Apparently not, to judge from Mallory's attitude.

"By the way, your statement is ready for your signature. We'd appreciate it if you would stop by the station to take care of it," he was saying. "Meanwhile, confine your inquiries to the doggies, and stay out of police business."

I smiled, determined to keep my temper. One never knew

when a friendly contact in the police department might come in handy.

"Don't worry," I said as I drove away. "I assure you, if it doesn't have four legs and a tail, I'm not interested."

7

Legwork

I SPENT THE rest of the morning distributing flyers in the Orange Blossom Heights area, tucking the neon-pink "lost dog" bulletins inside screen doors and under doormats, and stapling them to telephone poles and fence posts. The stapling was quite possibly in violation of some local ordinance, but I hoped to have Herbie back home and the flyers removed before anyone had time to complain.

It was while I was working Jessica's tree-lined cul-de-sac that I picked up my first clue. I parked my car in the shade of an old eucalyptus tree, then, starting out from Jessica's nearest neighbour, made my way up one side of the winding road and down the other, Watson walking sedately by my side. At the end of each driveway she would sit and wait patiently for me. I did not allow her to accompany me to the front door, for fear of provoking a confrontation with a resident dog. However, the most threatening encounter so far had been with a languid Basset hound who had watched my progress up and then back down his driveway with droopy-eyed indifference.

The last house we visited was almost directly across from Jessica's. A one-level ranch-style, a design popular in the fifties and sixties, the house was modest for the neighbourhood. I guessed that when it eventually came on the market it would be demolished and replaced with something more in keeping with its upscale neighbours. For now, however, the house held its ground, seemingly at peace with its peeling paint and chipped white stucco, the green roof missing a tile here and there. The front of the house was almost hidden by a tangle of shrubbery, dominated by yellow hibiscus, the large buttery cups flaunting pollen-flocked stamens at the ruby-throated hummingbirds darting in and out of the deep green foliage. One of the hummers buzzed by my ear, and I paused for a moment to admire its iridescent plumage, hoping it would perch and allow me to get a good look at it. But in response to my stare it abruptly changed gear and whirred off in another direction.

I stepped to the porch and was about to slip a flyer behind the unlocked screen when the front door opened slightly, and a greyish, lined face peered out.

"I told you the other day I'm not interested in your get-rich-quick schemes," a rasping voice said. I could not tell immediately whether the speaker was male or female.

"I'm not selling anything," I said, taken by surprise.

"Oh. Sorry. Saw the flyer and thought you was the woman who came by last week, promising me a big profit if I sold the house," the voice continued. "I told her, 'I've lived here thirty years, it's paid for, I'm comfortable, got enough to live on. Where the hell else would I go?' "

By this time the door had opened wide enough for me to see that the speaker was an elderly man, not much taller than me, or so it seemed from the way he crouched over a heavy walking stick, its wood polished to a high shine from years of use.

"No," I said. "I'm not a realtor. Actually, I'm looking for a lost dog." I offered him the flyer. "It belongs to your neighbour across the street, Mrs. Lomax. Have you seen it?"

He took the flyer from me, adjusted his glasses, then said, "Good riddance. Damn dogs, barking at all hours. The other night they woke me up. Made such a racket, I nearly called the cops.''

My interest quickened. "What night was that?''

"Last week sometime. Tuesday or Wednesday, think it was. Late anyway. Looked out the window and saw one of them pizza cars over there.'' He nodded toward Jessica's house. "Eating pizza that time of night,'' he sniffed. "Hope they got heartburn.''

"Did you recognize anyone?''

"Couple of young men came to her door. Never seen them before. They had that punk music playing real loud. What they call music, anyway.''

Jessica had made no mention of a second person staying there while she was away, I thought.

The old man chatted on. "Went over there a day or so later to complain to Mrs. Lomax, but no one was home. Could hear the dogs barking in back, though. They've been barking on and off all week. Been thinking about calling . . . er . . .'' He grasped for the right words. "What do you call the dogcatchers?''

"Animal control,'' I offered.

"That's right. Animal control.'' He nodded. "But when the cops showed up yesterday, I figured they'd take care of it.'' He paused, scratching a grey thatch of hair. "Did, too, I reckon. Haven't heard the dogs since.''

"That's because Mrs. Lomax is back now,'' I said. "Did you tell the police about the pizza delivery?'' I knew next to nothing about police procedure but thought it very likely that they would canvass the neighbourhood for just this kind of information.

"Took me too long to get out of bed when they knocked early this morning,'' he said. "By the time I got to the door they'd gone.'' His gnarled hand wobbled the walking stick as he spoke. "Arthritis, you know.''

I nodded sympathetically.

"They'll be back later on, I'm sure,'' I said, adding,

"Just one more thing. Did you happen to see the name of the pizza company?"

"No. Had a picture of a pizza on the car door, though. I remember that. Think there was a box of some sort alongside it, too. But the old eyes ain't what they used to be, you know."

"Well, I think you did very well. You've been a great help." I looked at my watch. "I mustn't keep you any longer. My telephone number is on the flyer. If you should see the dog, please give me a call, or tell Mrs. Lomax."

Nice old man. I hope he hangs on to his house, I thought as I dumped the remainder of the flyers in the back of the station wagon. Glad I ran into him. It would be very helpful in establishing the day of the murder, and therefore the most likely day that Herbie had run off, if I knew which night the pizza had been delivered.

. 8 .

One Good Turn...

ON MY WAY back to the freeway I made a detour through the business district, keeping my eyes peeled for pizza parlours. Waiting at a traffic light, I spotted a sign sporting a large pizzalike disc slowly spinning around a pole, which, on closer inspection, bore a passing resemblance to a record on a turntable. On investigation, however, I found that Pizza Platter was closed, a sign in the window indicating that they delivered on Fridays, Saturdays, and Sundays only.

I drove on, beginning to think that perhaps this was not the best way to go about things, that I should go home and work my way through the pizza listings in the yellow pages. I was, in fact, looking for the nearest freeway on-ramp when, on the opposite side of the street, I caught sight of a sign depicting a large pizza, together with a pair of dice. Could they be the ''box'' the old man had seen? I made a U-turn at the next traffic signal and shortly thereafter parked in front of Lotsa Lucky Pizza, hoping that the name would prove prophetic.

As I entered, the smell of pepperoni and melted cheese reminded me that I had left home without breakfast. I ordered a slice of gourmet veggie delite (bell peppers, mushrooms, onions, and zucchini) and a small diet drink, and asked to speak to the person in charge, selecting a table by the window so I could keep an eye on Watson, waiting in the car.

A pimply-faced youth whose name tag, I read with some astonishment, announced that he was Don, the assistant manager, approached. His slicked-down, close-trimmed hair, crisp white shirt, well-pressed black pants, and highly polished black shoes told me that here was a young man who took his job seriously.

"Is there a problem, ma'am?" he asked earnestly.

When questioned Don told me that yes, they made deliveries in the Orange Blossom Heights neighbourhood, and yes, he'd have to check, but he thought they had delivered there a couple of evenings last week.

I told him that I was looking for a dog lost in that area and was trying to trace back to when it had last been seen. I gave him the address, and with some hesitation, obviously not at all convinced that this was in his job description, he went to look up the orders for the previous week.

While I waited, I nibbled on my pizza, which, in reality, proved to be neither gourmet nor delightful. Oily cheese dripped onto the paper plate, the mushrooms tasted of plastic, the zucchini rubber. The old man's warning of heartburn echoed back to me.

The indigestion factor notwithstanding, it was a thriving little establishment. Lunchtime was approaching, and the telephone rang almost constantly, keeping the young woman assistant busy taking orders. Behind her the cook slammed pizzas in and out of the wide ovens, preparing for the noontime rush.

"Yes, ma'am." Don returned with the news that Lotsa Lucky had delivered to Jessica's house the previous Tuesday night.

"Who made the delivery?" I asked.

"That would have been Pete Kelley," Don said. "But he's not here right now."

"Oh, that's too bad," I said. "I was hoping I could speak to him. Could I have his telephone number?"

"Sorry. We're not allowed to give out personal information on our employees," said the assistant manager officiously, his tone quite at odds with his youthful appearance. "Anyway, I'm not sure he still works for us. Hasn't been in since, and the boss is sure getting mad."

I caught my breath. Could Pete be the young man I'd found dead in Jessica's doghouse? I pulled myself together and tried again.

"Well, here's my card," I said. "I would really appreciate it if you would have Pete give me a call when he shows up."

Don glanced at the card politely. "Delilah Doolittle, Pet Detective," he said slowly. "Hey, I know you. You're the one that found my grandmother's cat, Cupid, that time. Cool."

I remembered. I don't get many cat cases. Cats are difficult to trace and, like I said, people leave it too long before they start looking. But the name Cupid rang the proverbial bell. So called because of a black heart-shaped mark on the head of an otherwise all white cat. I had been lucky enough to spot him at the animal shelter a day or so after the owner contacted me. The woman was on Social Security, and it had been such an easy case, that I . . .

"Didn't charge her nothing, neither," said Don, breaking in on my recollection, a warm smile replacing his serious assistant manager expression. "Poor gran had been carrying on for days about that cat. Tell you what. I owe you one." He looked around conspiratorially, then, reaching into his pocket protector for a pen, hastily scribbled an address on the back of a paper menu.

"Doesn't have a phone," he said. "Lives in one of those apartments down by the pier. When he's not surfing, that is."

"How kind of you," I thanked him.

"No problemo. Gotta go," he said, already heading for a group of early lunchers who had just arrived.

BACK ON THE freeway, I switched on the radio just in time to hear a police spokesman saying, "... when the police arrived they found the body of an adult male, later identified as Steven Potter, of no fixed address, who had been hired by the owner of the house to take care of her pets during her absence."

No wonder Detective Mallory had been so suspicious of my visit to Jim Ratchett's earlier that morning.

9

Cross Words

"ONLY THE PATTIE," I told Watson. "No bun. You've got to cut down on the starch or you won't be able to get through the doggie door." Nothing for me. That slice of pizza would be enough to hold me until the Crab Louis luncheon I was anticipating later at Evie's expense.

We were in the park across the street from the Surf City police station, sitting on the grass in the shade of an ancient oak tree that, through some miracle, had escaped the developer's axe. I loved this part of town, with its early century charm, and old homes converted into attorneys' offices and interior decorators' showrooms. My favourite antique store and tearoom were located nearby. At another time I would have enjoyed browsing through the one and partaking of a leisurely pot of tea and a toasted tea cake in the other, but today there was no time for such indulgences.

I broke the hamburger into pieces, handing them to Watson one at a time—she would have bolted the pattie whole otherwise—and watched with casual interest the comings and goings across the street. Among the arrivals was a young woman, perhaps eighteen or nineteen years old, being escorted, weeping, into the station by one of the officers I had met at Jessica's the previous day.

I filled Watson's water bowl from the bottle I always carry in the car, poured some into a paper cup for myself, then, duly refreshed, hurried over to present myself at the station reception desk, prepared to sign my statement. I was a trifle apprehensive, and not a little curious, about what to expect, this being my first and, I trusted, last brush with the law. I inquired, hopefully, if Detective Mallory might be at lunch, wishing if at all possible to avoid a second encounter with him that day. He was not, and I was shown into his office where he had just finished eating. Now, Chinese take-away food cartons shoved aside, he was working the *Times* crossword puzzle.

It didn't take long to review and sign my account of the chain of events leading up to my discovery of the body, and I thought Mallory was about to send me on my way, when he said casually, as if he had only just thought of it, "How well do you know Anthony Tipton?"

"Anthony Tip . . . ?" I had to think for a minute before the name registered. He was talking about Tiptoe Tony.

"Don't deny you know him," he went on. "We have proof that he contacted you after he was brought in for questioning yesterday evening."

"I have no intention of denying knowing him," I said, shocked that he would think me capable of lying. "Though I'd hardly call him a friend. He lives near me at the beach, and I have helped him with his dog on a couple of occasions."

"Dogs again," he said dryly. "And I suppose you're going to tell me you know nothing about his involvement in the Steven Potter case."

Tony involved in a murder? Impossible. Guilty of petty theft, a con artist, maybe. But murder? How in the world did he get mixed up in this?

Aloud I said, "That's preposterous!"

"Then you know more than I do. All I know is his prints were found at the scene. And a neighbour who observed him at the house, knowing Mrs. Lomax was away, wrote down his registration number. A vanity plate, easy enough to remember. Tipton has been picked up for questioning. But then you know that.''

''I know nothing of the sort, and I wish you would stop insinuating otherwise.''

''Mrs. Doolittle,'' he went on in the most irritating and patronizing way, ''I would advise you to consider your words carefully. We have it on record that Tipton signed an order releasing his dog to you.''

''That is correct. I'm going to the shelter this afternoon. He left a message on my answering machine asking me to take care of the dog. But that's neither here nor there. It certainly doesn't mean I know anything about this other business.''

''So you mean to tell me that you were at the scene of the crime, discovered the body, in fact, and now a known felon who you admit associating with has been picked up in connection with that crime, and you know nothing about it?''

''I certainly do mean to tell you so.'' I was getting agitated, my face was burning. His use of the words ''associating with'' suggested some kind of sinister alliance. And I was beginning to feel more than a little put out with Tony for, however unwittingly, being the cause of my discomfort. ''Furthermore,'' I continued, ''I mean to tell you that I'm getting tired of your insinuations . . .'' I broke off. ''It's 'Shiba Inu.' ''

''What?'' Mallory looked puzzled.

''Five down. Small Japanese dog. Eight letters.'' I had done the crossword myself over tea that morning, so it was no great trick to read it upside down. And I gained a certain satisfaction in the thought that, if he was like me, he would detest having crossword solutions given him gratuitously.

''Never heard of that one. How do you spell it?'' He took it quite graciously, but the twinge of conscience I felt at having stooped to such petty one-upmanship was quickly replaced by irritation at having been put in this position in the first place.

I spelled it out for him, then, while he jotted down the letters, took the opportunity to ask if the time of Steven Potter's death had yet been established.

Again caught off guard, he replied tersely, "We're still waiting for the coroner's report. Why?"

"Well, it occurs to me we may be able to help each other. Your job is to find the murderer. Mine is to find the dog. I think the two might be connected. If the dog ran off during the murder, it would help if I knew how long he's been gone."

Far from offering to keep me informed, Detective Mallory responded with words to the effect that the last person he might seek help from would be a pet detective, and, once again admonishing me to leave the detecting to the authorities, he bid me good afternoon and returned to his crossword.

I was sure there was a tart and witty rejoinder to this, but unfortunately nothing satisfactory came immediately to mind. Fuming at his stubbornness, and frustrated at not having had the last word, I made my way back to the lobby. There all thoughts of verbal retaliation vanished when, as luck would have it, I came face-to-face with the sister of the deceased.

• 10 •

Delilah Meets Debbie

HER EYES RED with tears, the girl I had observed entering the police station earlier was now being escorted out by Officer Perkins, the younger of the two policemen I had met at Jessica's. He was doing his embarrassed best to comfort her, trying awkwardly to pat her shoulder and proffering a battered box of tissues. I gave him a sympathetic smile and, as he seemed to be at somewhat of a loss, said, "Is there anything I can do?"

He looked relieved. "Mrs. Doolittle. Er, this is Debbie Potter, Steven's sister."

Instinctively I put out my hand to comfort her.

Her dishwater-blond hair, moussed into spikes, exclaimed over pencil-thin eyebrows, which in turn headlined pale blue eyes awash in a sad mix of blue eye shadow, mascara, and tears.

Her outfit, set off by a pair of black granny boots, was more appropriate for a stroll along the pier than a visit to the police station. Denim cutoff shorts and a cropped-top boob tube left nothing to the imagination, though she was so skinny, there wasn't much to imagine. The wince I felt on observing the jewelled stud in her nose, as she dabbed at it with a damp tissue, deepened as my gaze was drawn to the matching gem in her navel. As one who could never bear to contemplate even getting my ears pierced, much less any other part of my anatomy, I had to admire her courage. How did these young people endure the pain?

"Sit here for a minute or two," the officer was telling her, indicating a wooden bench, "and I'll see about a ride home for you."

I looked at my watch. I still had an hour before meeting Evie.

"I'm just leaving, Officer," I said. "I'd be glad to give Debbie a ride home." My offer was not entirely altruistic. Maybe, if I broached the subject delicately enough, she might be able to give me some details of her brother's pet-sitting schedule last week.

Debbie looked at me directly for the first time and managed a weak smile. "Thanks," she said. "I don't want my landlady to see me coming home in a cop car." Handing the tissue box back to young Officer Perkins with an appraising glance that suggested that grief had not entirely overcome her interest in the opposite sex, she accompanied me out to the street.

Watson, alerted by our approach, stood up as I opened the car door. Debbie hesitated. "That your dog?"

I was prepared for this reaction. Watson does look rather intimidating. "She won't hurt you, Debbie," I reassured her.

"I'm not scared. I'm used to dogs. But I don't like Dobies. My uncle uses them in his work. They're, like, totally mean."

"Well, I think it depends on how they're treated," I said, recalling her uncle's objectionable training methods. "Watson's a pussycat." Intent on proving the truth of this, Watson clambered onto the front seat between us and sat with her chin on my shoulder.

I held off from saying anything about pet sitting or missing dogs for the time being, for fear of setting off a further torrent of tears. If it occurred to Debbie to wonder what I was doing at the police station, she didn't mention it.

Before long she started to cry again. Watson, turning her big head toward her, began to lick away the tears. Debbie managed a bleak smile.

"I don't understand it. Like, why would anyone want to kill Steve?" she sniffled as we drove toward her home in Westgrove, a low-rent community located on the edge of town. Why indeed? I was hoping she might have some information that would help us find an answer to that one.

"Had Steven done much pet sitting?" I asked.

"No. Uncle Jim was supposed to be doing the Lomax job, because she's an old friend of his, but something came up and Steve ended up doing it. He was working so hard. Uncle Jim said that if he, like, straightened out he could be in charge of the, you know, the sentry dogs." I wondered what it was that Steven needed to straighten out from. She took a pack of Marlboro Lights from her denim backpack, her hands trembling as she lit up. I pointedly rolled down my window but refrained from comment. Watson quit her tear-licking, sneezed, and climbed into the backseat.

"You don't have a car?" I asked.

"No. Me and Steve use one of Uncle's trucks sometimes. Or my friends take me places." This gave me the opening I needed to ask about something that had been bothering me.

"How did Steven get to work?" I hadn't seen any sign of what might have been his transportation when I was at Jessica's the previous day.

"One of the trucks was in the shop, and Uncle needed the other one, so a friend dropped Steve off at Mrs. Lomax's last weekend. Like, if he needed a ride or anything he would just call someone. But he told me Mrs. Lomax had left plenty of stuff in the fridge so he didn't need much. And he liked being in that nice big house all by himself."

"So you didn't see him after he left for Mrs. Lomax's at the beginning of last week?"

"Well, yes. One night, I think it was Tuesday, a friend brought him by."

At the thought of her last meeting with Steven, the tears started to flow again, so I refrained from any further questions, and we completed the journey in a silence broken only by her snuffled directions to the ground-floor apartment she shared with Steven and a girlfriend.

The apartment building was located on a street of similar structures, each indistinguishable from its neighbours except for the colour of the stucco, the number of "apartment for rent" signs blossoming on the hanky-sized front lawns, and the plants used in what could only loosely be described as landscaping. The apartments in Debbie's building were centered around a courtyard complete with a kidney-shaped pool, sorely in need of a good scouring. The apartments on the upper floors had small balconies, those on the ground floor tiny enclosed patios.

I was prepared to drop Debbie off at the curb, but I readily accepted when she invited me in to show me a picture of Steven. It seemed unkind to refuse, and there still might be something useful she could tell me about her brother. Leaving Watson in the car, in the shade of some dusty pink and white oleanders, I followed Debbie in.

The apartment was a mess, but no more so than I would have expected for three young people living together, each leaving the niceties of dish-washing, ashtray emptying, tidying, dusting, and cleaning to the other. The small living room was stifling, the windows tightly closed. Cigarette smoke hung in the air, clung to the shabby drapes.

I stepped outside for a breather while Debbie went to get the picture. The sloppy housekeeping extended to the patio. A barbeque with the congealed remains of a weekend cookout still clinging to the grill attracted flies. Likewise, food had hardened around the rim of a plastic pet dish, while a water bowl displayed a thin film of green slime.

"Do you have a pet?" I asked as she came out onto the patio with the photograph.

"No. Steven was watching a dog for a friend, okay? But it ran away yesterday. I was, like, going to look for it this morning when the police came. It'll come back when it's hungry." Such callous indifference in one so young bothered me, but I immediately dismissed the thought as uncharitable, considering her grief-stricken condition. It was only in the past few hours the poor child had learned that her brother had been brutally murdered.

"You might check the shelter over on Central Avenue," I suggested. "Do you know where it is, by the freeway? In fact," I went on, "I'm going there myself later this afternoon. If you want to give me a description, I'll watch out for the dog."

"No, that's okay," she said offhandedly. "My roommate can take me when she gets home." I had my doubts. She seemed singularly unconcerned, and anxious to change the subject. "This is Steve," she said, handing me a cheap metal picture frame.

The photograph, actually an enlargement of a slightly out-of-focus snapshot, showed Debbie and her brother at the beach. The family resemblance was remarkable. Their mother had been Uncle Jim's sister, she said. Steven was a younger version of his uncle. Skinny. A matchstick with the wood scraped off, my mother would have said. A can of beer in one hand, a cigarette hanging out of his mouth, an arm draped across Debbie's shoulders, almost as if she were supporting him. As well she might have been from the looks of him.

Looking at the picture set her off sobbing again.

"Do you have a friend we can call?" I asked. I was reluctant to leave her, but Evie would be waiting.

"That's okay." She glanced forlornly at the ticktock cat on the wall. "My roommate will be home from work soon. Thanks for the ride, though."

With that she switched on the television, already tuned to MTV, lit up another cigarette, and started moving around the room in rhythm with the music.

I set off for the railway station marveling once again, as so often in the past, at the resilience of the human spirit.

. 11 .

Evie Joins the Fray

WITH ITS SPANISH-style architecture, tiled roof, and paved arcades, the century-old Surf City railway depot is a relic of a more leisurely era. For decades it languished in disuse, but in recent years Amtrak, prompted by the need to get people out of their cars and into public transit, had revitalized the southern California rail system, and the depot, spruced up with an eye to its heritage, had become a daily departure point for hundreds of commuters.

It was barely half past one when I arrived, and I was glad to have a few minutes to look around before Evie got there. I had travelled much in my earlier years, but terminals, whether bus, train, or air, still had the power to excite me. Mundane daily routines give way to the demands of ETAs, ETDs, electronic bulletin boards, and unintelligible public address systems. A sense of excitement pervades the air; people coming and going somewhere, anywhere, which must, by definition, be more exciting than wherever one is. I longed to be part of it again. I picked up a timetable and slipped it in my purse. On my next visit to Evie, I would take the train.

Evie's train arrived right on time. I observed her ample but stylishly dressed figure a moment or two before she spied me. She was wearing a white linen pantsuit, with yellow trim, and a shiny white straw cloche. Even in casual California, for Evie hats are *de rigueur*. With a hat, she declares, there's no such thing as a bad hair day.

"Do you like the hat, sweetie?" she asked as we kissed air. "That makes twenty-six. Summer, that is. God only knows how many winter."

She gave me an appraising look, and I belatedly realized that in my haste I had forgotten to freshen my lipstick after the pizza, and that, compared to hers, my outfit left much to be desired. I silently agreed with her when she declared in clarion tones that I looked an "absolute rag."

In one hand she carried a smashing designer overnight case, in the other a rather indifferent-looking zippered sport bag.

"I'm absolutely gasping for a ciggie," she said as soon as we reached the outside courtyard, stopping in the shade of an ancient oak tree to light up. "Can you imagine, no smoking allowed on the train?" She put down the sport bag while groping in the portmanteau for her cigarettes.

"What's in the sport bag?" I asked.

"Oh. I almost forgot. It's the dog. He's such a quiet little thing." Reaching into the bag she extracted a tiny and rather bewildered white dog. This was Chamois, Evie's mop of a Maltese. His hair pulled back out of his eyes with a jewelled barrette, he wore an expression of constant astonishment. As well he might. Evie was someone to be constantly astonished at.

"Doggies are not allowed on trains, either, sweetie. Did you ever hear such nonsense? But we don't care about their silly rules, do we, my treasure?" she said, planting a lip-sticky kiss on the dog's already pink head. "Couldn't leave him behind, could I? It would break his little heart, bless him." The dog blinked button black eyes at her through the ciggie smoke.

Leaving me to pick up her bags, she headed out to the parking lot, dog in one hand and cigarette in the other, rattling on in nonstop fashion about one thing then another, until we reached the car.

Now she was talking about the train ride. "I think one should try everything once," she said. "And I think it's about time you tried buying a new car," she added, stepping cautiously into the wagon. "My Mercedes man's a gem. He could get you a really good buy. Seriously."

"Seriously," I said, "gems are not in my budget."

It was only a short distance to the Mountain View Lodge where we were to lunch. Evie was right. It was a favourite of mine, particularly since the alfresco dining allowed Watson and Chamois to join us.

Evie eyed the menu speculatively. "I'd better not eat too much," she said. "I've been sitting all morning, and I've got the drive back." That said, she ordered the lobster Newburg, clam chowder, and "Oh, some of those delightful popovers you do so well here, sweetie," she said to the waitress, who appeared a little taken aback by Evie's flamboyance.

I, on the other hand, was too nervous to eat. Evie had me on edge, and the cumulative effects of the events of yesterday and today had robbed me of my appetite. Foregoing the promised Crab Louis, I settled for the spinach salad.

"You're just trying to make me look like a piggy," Evie said.

While we ate, we brought each other up-to-date on our lives since the last time we'd met—her recent trip to Minorca, mine to the car repair shop—and I filled her in on my latest caper. When I got to the part about finding the body in the doghouse, she exclaimed with a shudder, "How absolutely ghastly. You really do know the most extraordinary people."

I smarted at the implied criticism but held my tongue. I allowed her, as my oldest friend, a certain amount of attitude that I would never have tolerated from anyone else.

Later, while I finished my coffee, Evie made her way to

the lobby to telephone the car dealership and make sure her car was ready.

I fed the last of my roll to the birds sitting on the backs of the chairs waiting for handouts. Generations of sparrows and finches had been raised in the shelter of this pleasant courtyard, and they were as tame as parakeets. As far as they knew, this was the life nature had intended for them.

I petted Chamois and thought about Evie. We had been friends since school in England, and it had been an unlikely alliance from the start. She was a privileged only child from a titled family. I was attending the private school on a scholarship. She was chauffeured to school daily; I took the bus. One day, as I waited at the bus stop in the pouring rain, she had stopped and offered me a ride. "How perfectly beastly for you," she had said, amazed to learn that the bus was my only mode of transport. And thus was born a friendship which has long outlasted our school days. Our paths had paralleled ever since, both of us travelling to California in our adventurous youth, later marrying here. There the similarities ended. She had married well. I was widowed early, now getting by on a shoestring income.

Evie's car wasn't ready. "Dreadful man," she said of the man who, only an hour earlier, had been an absolute gem. "I called last evening particularly to confirm I could pick up the car this afternoon, and now he tells me it won't be ready until tomorrow morning. I'll just have to stay with you tonight."

Blast, I thought, conscious that this was a slightly ungenerous reaction to my best friend's need for shelter for the night. But my plans for the afternoon definitely did not include Evie. Another time, I would have enjoyed her company for shopping or a film, but today I had work that couldn't wait. I outlined my schedule and offered to drop her off at South Coast Plaza, our smart shopping mall, if she didn't want to come along.

"Really, Dee," she said, opting to accompany me, "if you must work, I wish you would get yourself a real job.

All this running around after dogs and getting mixed up with the police. It's just not on. I worry about you.''

It was useless to explain that this was a real job, one for which sometimes, though rarely, as in the case of clients like Jessica Lomax, I got paid quite handsomely. And she would never understand that I really enjoyed the work. No time clock, plenty of fresh air, the company of animals. And anyway, I was not mixed up with the police, just ''assisting them in their inquiries,'' as they say in England.

It was not the first time we'd had this conversation, or a variation thereof, and it wouldn't be the last, but I didn't let it bother me. I knew in her own way Evie wanted the best for me. And the best, in her opinion was . . .

She picked up my train of thought. ''. . . a nice man,'' she was saying. ''Heaven knows, I've introduced you to enough, but you're not making any effort. You've still got your looks, and if I had your figure . . .'' She broke off, lost in a dreamworld of shopping, no doubt.

In the unaccustomed silence that followed I took the opportunity to say, perhaps a little more sharply than I ought, ''That's all well and good, but for now I've got commitments, and people are depending on me. Let's go.'' And picking up Watson's leash I headed off to the parking lot, leaving a surprised Evie to pick up Chamois, his carryall, and the bill.

· 12 ·

Something Sordid

THE NEXT TRICK was to get Evie in and out of the animal shelter without her adopting something. For all her sophistication, she was a softie at heart. She and Howard treated Chamois like the child they'd never had, and while she would say she chose the little dog because his colour matched her carpet, the real reason was because he was on death row when she had accompanied me to this same shelter a few years ago.

By a curious quirk of fate, or perhaps a streak of black humour on the part of some long-forgotten urban planner, the jail and the animal shelter were located next to each other and shared the same visitor parking lot.

I thought of the irony of Tony and Trixie locked up so near to each other. It must have been late yesterday evening when they had arrived together, only to be separated, he to go to his lockup, she to hers.

Leaving Evie to browse the "dogs available" cages, I made my way to where the police holds were housed. An additional barricade secured this area, whether to protect a curious public or to prevent a canine jailbreak had never been clear.

I located Trixie, nose pointed forlornly toward the gate,

awaiting deliverance along with other unfortunates who, like her, were in custody through no fault of their own, but because of the transgressions of their owners. Also incarcerated in this section were a couple of battle-scarred pit bulls impounded from illegal dogfights; and a Chow, a Shar-pei, and, surprise, a cocker spaniel, all quarantined for bites. They would have their day in court, I hoped. Who knew what circumstances lay behind their decision to react with the only weapon available to them, their teeth.

A quick survey of the shelter showed nothing remotely resembling a Herbert Fitzherbert, so while at the office claiming Trixie, I asked Rita if she would check her records for German shepherds that might have been picked up dead or were being treated by outside veterinarians. Shelter policy required that animal control officers take seriously injured animals to the closest vet for treatment.

Rita's pink acrylic nails picked deftly through the past few days' DOA and vet intake reports. There was nothing. She looked at the clock; it was near closing time.

"The trucks will be here in a few minutes," she said. "Why don't you go out to station three and see what they bring in."

An animal's progression through the shelter is marked by four main areas, or stations. It enters either through station one, the main gate, or is off-loaded from a truck at station three. Its impound records are filed at station two, the office. There are only two ways for an animal to exit: through station one, having been reunited with its owner or adopted by a new family; or through station four, the clinic, where the sick, the badly injured, or otherwise unadoptable are painlessly euthanized by lethal injection. The people who perform this sad task are among the most compassionate I know, sending each animal on its way with gentle hands and a kind word, maybe the only one they have ever heard in their unhappy lives.

I found Evie looking pensively at an overweight and morose Boston terrier. I had to remind her that she was soon to drive back to San Diego in a brand-new car and perhaps a dog of dubious habits might not be the best travelling companion.

"But nobody's going to adopt such a pathetic-looking creature," Evie protested.

Fortunately she was relieved of any pangs of conscience concerning this particular dog by a sudden outburst of "Sugarbaby, I've found you," from an elderly woman who had just entered the area. That the Boston terrier was hers there was no doubt. At the sound of her voice it wobbled to its feet and yapped excitedly. If any doubt remained, one had only to look at the pair of them. Their striking resemblance to each other, even to the dark protruding eyes, squat round face, and short dumpy figure, was proof enough that they belonged together. The woman's outfit of black skirt, white blouse, and black vest completed the match. A thought: Do pets and owners acquire each other's characteristics as the companion animal bond deepens through the years? I have observed this phenomenon too often for it to be mere coincidence. Or perhaps it's just that people tend to select pets that carry a certain reflection of themselves.

Evie and I returned to station three and watched as the animal control officers unloaded their trucks, skillfully removing their bewildered cargo from individual compartments, completing paperwork, checking license tags, and scanning for microchip IDs before placing the dogs in the appropriate kennel area. Seldom did they find it necessary to resort to the catch-pole—a long pole with a noose at the end—used to control the more aggressive or skittish animals. Tranquilizer guns were employed even more rarely, only when all other methods had failed, or when human life was at risk, as in the case of trespassing wildlife. Such had been the case today, Rita had told me. A bobcat that had wandered into a backyard in south county had been captured and later released in the Cleveland National Forest by Lt. Mike Denver, the senior animal control officer.

Mike had just returned to the shelter. Waiting until he

had locked the tranquilizer gun away in a cabinet behind the clinic, I called, "Hi, there." Mike was an old friend. I had known him since he was taken on as a kennel attendant here, fresh out of high school, and had watched with a certain amount of proprietary interest his progress up through the ranks into handsome and capable manhood. He and Rita had recently announced their engagement. I couldn't be more pleased. They were a delightful couple.

"Hi, Delilah. What're you after today?" I handed him a Herbie flyer and asked him to pass the word along.

"No problem," he said. He took a bunch more flyers to hand out to his officers and, offering to pin one on the bulletin board by the main gate, accompanied us out for this purpose.

As we left, with Trixie in tow, we bumped into the lady with the Boston terrier. "How can I ever thank you," she said to Mike. "You saved her life."

"No problem," Mike said again. The overworked phrase was, regrettably, a favourite of his. Though he, probably more than most, meant it when he said it. "Just doing my job." He really was a most obliging chap. He pinned the flyer to the bulletin board and returned to the yard.

As we made our way to the car park, Sugarbaby's owner told us that Mike had been the officer who had picked up the dog on busy Main Street during rush hour. The dog had escaped through a backyard gate carelessly left open by a meter reader, and would surely have been run over if Mike hadn't taken care of her.

A happy ending for us to contemplate on the drive home. Trixie, who finally got the hint that Watson was not the least bit interested in her friendly overtures, and sensing the opportunity for a cuddle, selected Evie's ample lap as the most comfortable place for the ride, Chamois being tucked safely away in his sport bag, resting at Evie's feet.

We arrived home. As soon as I got out of the car I saw that the front door was ajar. I'm one of those self-doubters who compulsively check two or three times before leaving the house, so I knew the door was locked when I left. Now what? I thought. And whatever it is, why does it have to be now, with Evie here?

I tentatively pushed the door open a little further, and let Watson go in ahead of me. After a couple of minutes, hearing no warning bark, we followed her in.

"My God, Dee, this place is a tip," Evie said in disgust, surveying what surely not even the worst of housekeepers would countenance.

I didn't know if I would rather her think that this was the way I lived, or have her know that my home had been broken into. But she could see for herself. Sofa pillows were ripped, drawers turned out, everything swept off cupboard shelves.

"Dee. Really. Now I shall insist you move. I told you I didn't like you living here. You're too close to the criminal element." She, like me, assumed that the break-in was the work of young vandals. School was still out, and being so close to the beach, my house no doubt offered an easy mark. With Watson around I had never feared for my safety before. Now I wasn't so sure. I did not scare easily, but after the events of yesterday and now this, I was beginning to feel vulnerable.

I picked up the telephone in the living room to call the police. Evie, who had been "gasping for a cup of tea, sweetie," ever since we left the shelter, went into the kitchen to put on the kettle.

Too late I remembered that in my rush out the door this morning I hadn't emptied the teapot. I heard her at the sink. "Dee," she called. "Don't you have any decent tea? These used tea bags are gross, they look like drowned mice."

Evie was a purist when it came to tea; only the finest loose, imported was good enough for her. I, on the other hand, had long since abandoned tradition for convenience.

I started to dial again.

"Dee," she called. "I think you should come here . . ."

Now what? Was she going to insist on demonstrating the

similarities between my sodden tea bags and waterlogged rodents? I really was not in the mood. I put down the phone and looked up. She was standing in the doorway, my brown Betty teapot in trembling hand, her flawless complexion as white as her hat, now slightly askew.

"Do come look," she said. "There's something sordid under the sink."

· 13 ·

Constable!

I DON'T KNOW how it is in other households, but in my house "something sordid under the sink" might be anything from a rancid dishrag to a hair ball left by the transient tomcat who occasionally had the temerity to access the kitchen via Watson's doggie door.

What it actually turned out to be, however, was an infantile but nonetheless unpleasant attempt to warn me off my quest for Herbie. Sitting atop the garbage pail was Watson's teddy bear, a note impaled on its chest with a small vegetable knife. The note was splotched with something that suggested blood but on closer inspection turned out to be ketchup from one of those annoying little packets that come with take-away food, thrown out last night along with the hamburger wrappings. The message read:

If you don't want to get hurt, forget Herbie Lomax.

Exasperation vied with fear as I groped for an inkling of who could have done such a stupid thing.

"What does it mean? And who is Herbie Lomax?" asked Evie, frowning nervously. I reminded her that Herbie was the dog in the case I was working on.

"What shall we do with it?" she said.

I held the offending bear at arm's length. "Could be

wired. Better call the bomb squad,'' I said, trying to make light of the situation for Evie's sake.

"Don't be fatuous, dear, it doesn't become you."

"Well, I refuse to take such childish threats seriously." I was attempting to play down this odd occurrence in an effort to alleviate Evie's distress, and also to head off the inevitable renewed efforts to get me into another line of work.

I completed my call to the police from the phone in the kitchen, while a somewhat subdued Evie, for once relatively speechless, retired to the living room with the tea tray. Our late lunch had left neither one of us with an appetite for dinner, and tea and biscuits was all we fancied at the moment. Which was just as well. Apart from an ample supply of dog food, my cupboard was exceedingly bare.

It had been a long and tiring day, and would be even more so by the time the police had come and gone.

I passed the time waiting for their arrival by verifying that nothing of value had been taken. In fact, the more I thought about it, the more the whole thing looked like vandalism, pure and simple, and I might have dismissed it as such if it hadn't been for the note.

I checked the doggie door, which was somewhat large to accommodate Watson. It was still bolted. No forced entry there. Then, in the back spare bedroom, I found a smashed window. The yard outside the window was overgrown with trees and shrubbery, and would have provided plenty of cover for an intruder during the day, when most of the neighbours were at work.

The dogs, meanwhile, were in the process of establishing their canine pecking order. Watson and Trixie had regarded each other with ill-concealed hostility on the drive home, and now that it had become obvious that Tony's Jack Russell terrier was to be an overnight guest, Watson displayed not the least interest in playing the cordial hostess. She guarded her food dish, and even growled Trixie off when she approached the water bowl. Little Chamois they both regarded with disdain as not worthy of the challenge.

The law finally arrived in the ungainly shape of Officer Offley, who had been the first uniform on the scene at Jessica's the previous day.

"So, Mrs. Doolittle, tracer of missing pets. What is it this time?" he said gruffly, his heavy features set in stern lines as he flipped open his notebook with elaborate officiousness.

Watson and Trixie, in a rare show of unity, took immediate offense to his tone, and each in her own way expressed their dislike of the newcomer: Trixie, by preliminary inspection of his trouser leg, Watson in the more conventional curled lip, check-out-these-teeth manner.

"Trixie! Watson! No," I commanded half-heartedly. They could read my mind, however, and continued to misbehave. Neither Evie nor I bothered to discourage them further.

Shaking his leg in a vain attempt to get rid of Trixie, Offley toured the house to see for himself the evidence of the break-in.

I had decided it might be better not to say anything about the note, but before I had a chance to tip off Evie, she was saying, "And to top it all off, we find this rubbishy note, threatening God knows what." She handed him the bear, with the note still affixed.

He might not have recollected who Herbie was, but the name Lomax definitely got his attention.

"I thought you were advised to stay out of police business, Mrs. Doolittle," he said dourly.

"That's all very well," I replied. "But I've done nothing to warrant this intrusion into my home. All I'm doing is looking for a lost dog. I'm more than happy to let you take care of the murderer. But I'm beginning to think there may be some connection between the murder and the missing dog."

"That's just the sort of muddled thinking we expect from

you humaniacs," he huffed, using the misnomer that the poorly informed were wont to apply to anyone even moderately concerned with the welfare of animals. The fact that he was not only applying the term unjustly, but using it incorrectly, was extremely aggravating. But I let it slide. I was too tired, upset, and distracted to debate animal rights ideology at this point. Besides, with this man I would be wasting my breath. Clearly, Officer Offley was one of those individuals who, having caught on to a good word or phrase, would hug it to him to the grave.

"People don't kill each other over dogs," he was saying. "I'm warning you, Mrs. Doolittle. Just stay out of it, or I'll have to arrest you for interfering with a police investigation." His community relations skills left a lot to be desired.

I was about to retort that I had in this case "stayed out of it," but that "it" had invaded my home, when Evie, seldom at a loss for words, and now fortified with tea, spoke up.

"Now, look here, Constable." She always rallied to my defense, even when, as now, I'd prefer to do without her help. "I won't have you talking to my friend that way. Kindly try to do your job without being offensive." She had never been known for her tact.

His expression unreadable, Offley turned to Evie. "Name, please."

"I don't believe we've been introduced. I'm Evelyn Cavendish, Mrs. Howard Cavendish." This last uttered in some expectation that he would recognize her important social standing in a community a hundred miles to the south.

He might have been forgiven for missing the connection even if he had been a devotee of the society pages. Right now Evie hardly looked the part of society matron. Her hat askew, white linen suit splotched with an abstract design of muddy paw prints, ketchup, and tea stains, her appearance was far from elegant.

"And are you a tracer of missing pets, also?" Offley inquired with heavy sarcasm.

"Don't be absurd," was as much as she allowed herself to say, perhaps realizing belatedly that now was not the time to ride her high horse.

He regarded her with bemusement for a moment longer, then turned his attention to the situation at hand.

Actually, since I could report nothing stolen, and the only evidence of a break-in was an upturned house and a mortally wounded teddy bear, there really wasn't much for him to do. Having confirmed he had all the details, he prepared to leave.

Turning to Evie, he said, "My advice to you, Mrs. Cavendish, is the same as I gave your friend here. Leave the investigating to the police." By this time Trixie was chewing on his pant leg in earnest. "And keep this damned dog under control, or I'll cite you for harbouring a vicious animal." He was obviously under the impression that the terrier belonged to Evie.

"Odious man," she said as the door closed behind him. "He provoked me intentionally. Just being bloody-minded, threatening to run you in. He was deliberately winding me up." She plumped down on the couch and poured herself another cup of tea.

Trixie, sensing an ally, jumped into her lap, spilling the tea as she did so.

Evie was not having a good day.

· 14 ·

Dog Beach

"REALLY, DEE, YOU are the limit, dragging me into this dreadful affair. I was looking forward to a nice leisurely day with you. I end up being attacked by dogs, harassed by the police, and quite scared out of my wits by threatening notes. I refuse to visit you again until you get this business cleared up and find yourself another line of work. I shall see what Howard can do for you." Evie's parting words when I dropped her off at the Mercedes dealer the following morning had shown just how little she understood my situation.

"Hang on a sec," I said, about to respond that I didn't drag her into anything, she came of her own accord. But before I could get the words out, she had put her smart new car in gear and was off in a huff back to San Diego.

I'd had quite enough of other people for a while—irate friends, hostile contacts, sarcastic policemen, and tearful bereaved. I needed some peace and quiet in which to sort through the events of the past two days; I needed fresh air to clear my head, and more than anything else, I needed tranquility to restore my spirits. Watson, Trixie, and I headed for the beach.

Dog Beach comes by its name honestly. It is the only

stretch along the ten-mile strand within the city limits where dogs are allowed. In earlier days access had been a scramble down the rough cliffside, and the beach itself, with its jagged rocks and pockets of tar, was the city's least attractive. But during a renovation to smooth away the rough edges of the city's character in a misguided and only partially successful attempt to emulate neighbouring Newport and Laguna, the walk above the cliffs had been landscaped, and a stairway and paved parking installed. Ironically, now that Dog Beach was no longer an eyesore, efforts had been made to ban dogs from this section also. Complaints of dog fights, and unscooped poop, and concern about bites, had assailed the city council from newcomers who, having purchased high-priced homes across Pacific Coast Highway, wanted the beach pristine and clinical, and would have banned the very seagulls given half a chance.

Dog owners retaliated in protest; beleaguered city fathers compromised. Dogs could continue to use the beach, but leashed only. It wasn't the same. Half the fun of taking your dog to the beach was to throw sticks into the ocean and watch her prance with doggy *joie de vivre* through the surf.

Unfortunately, some dog owners chose to ignore the mutt mitt dispensers at the foot of the cliff steps, and canine calling cards remained a hazard. But one of the many interesting snippets of folklore my mother had handed down to me was that it was lucky to step in dog poop. Later I realized that it was her way of comforting my embarrassment. But the lessons we learn in our formative years tend to stay with us throughout life, and if excursions to Dog Beach were anything to judge by, I must be the luckiest person alive.

On busy weekends and during the summer, most people observed the leash law. But if there weren't many beachgoers about, and there was no sign of the dog police, some of us still let our dogs run loose. Watson was not about to get into a fight, however provoked, and her toilet habits were impeccable. Trixie I wasn't so sure about, so I kept her securely on her leash.

Farther down the beach I could hear another dog barking joyously in play with its owner. The piercing screech of seagulls squabbling around a fire pit echoed above the relentless crash of the surf. I wondered idly if seagulls had altered genetically over the years as their diet had changed from sea fare to picnic leftovers.

I picked up a piece of driftwood, intending to throw it into the waves for Watson, but hesitated, reluctant to disturb the sandpipers at the shoreline. It was low tide, the best feeding time, and I didn't want them to miss a meal. I threw the stick down the beach instead.

Was it only two days since I had found the body in Jessica's doghouse? It seemed more like two weeks. Since then I'd twice been interviewed by the police, visited Jim Ratchett's place and Debbie's apartment, lunched with Evie, had her stay the night, been to the animal shelter, had my home broken into, and I had virtually nothing to show for any of it. One way or another, I was having trouble staying in touch with my primary objective: to find Herbie.

The simplest explanation was that the dog had run off in a panic during the murder. Despite my protestations to the contrary, I wasn't entirely convinced that Steven Potter had been done in over a dog. Maybe Officer Offley was right. People don't kill each other over dogs.

Or do they?

Stay out of it, warned the police. Stay out of it, warned the note. Stay out of what? I wondered. I was being warned off something of which I was unaware, not only by the police but by person or persons unknown who, for whatever reason, didn't want Herbie found.

Someone, maybe the murderer, was trying to scare me off the case, and they were doing a good job—up to a point. I was alarmed, but not enough to give up. Last night as I tossed and turned on my lumpy put-you-up (with the spare bedroom window broken, I'd let Evie have my room), it had crossed my mind to call Jessica and tell her I was refunding the retainer. But I needed the job. And was I a pet detective or wasn't I? Moreover, I certainly wasn't going to give Evie the satisfaction of thinking that she had convinced me to quit. Nor Detective Mallory and that oaf Offley, come to that. But I would have to be on my guard.

Trixie strained at the leash, desperate to join Watson in the chase for the stick.

I considered the people involved. Who might be a killer? Jim Ratchett could kill with a look, never mind a dog collar. But why would he kill his own nephew? Maybe he stole Herbie, and Steven found out. But the type of dog Ratchett was after could be obtained for twenty-five dollars at the shelter any day of the week. No, much as I would like to pin the whole thing on Ratchett, I had to admit it didn't seem very likely.

I found a not-too-uncomfortable rock and sat for a while enjoying the warm sun and the offshore breeze. A convoy of pelicans cruising low over the waves drew my attention to a school of dolphins heading in the same direction. Tony had once told me that sometimes dolphins would bodysurf alongside the surfers. How wonderful. It was almost enough to get me to take up surfing. Almost, but not quite. I found the water too cold. One of the few disappointments I had experienced on arriving in California was that the Pacific Ocean in these parts seldom gets above seventy-five degrees, even in the summer.

As I gazed at the surf, my thoughts returned to the crime. Maybe Steven had been in some kind of trouble. His sister had hinted as much, and perhaps Herbie's disappearance had nothing at all to do with the murder. But then, why the note?

The fact that it had referred to "Herbie" suggested a familiarity with the dog. A stranger might have said the "Lomax dog." A breeder, perhaps having stolen the dog out of jealousy or who-knows-what, might have said "Herbert Fitzherbert."

It was like a stereogram, one of those 3-D pictures that if you hold it at the end of your nose and cross your eyes you can see a hidden picture. If I could just peer beyond the confusing images I would be able to see the truth. And when I did I would see Herbie, and I would see Steven Potter's murderer.

Watson returned with the driftwood, and I aimlessly threw it for her again. Trixie, in a frenzy to join in the game, dragged me to my feet, and we trotted after Watson.

My thoughts turned from Steven to his sister. I'd hardly had time to give Debbie a second thought since Evie's arrival.

I had a sense that there was something I had missed on my visit with her. I thought about the airless apartment, the untidy living room, the tiny patio where she had shown me Steven's photograph. The greasy barbeque grill, the pet dishes . . .

I stopped in my tracks so suddenly that poor Trixie was jerked back in mid-stride. The friend's missing dog Debbie had told me about. Was that what had been hidden in the stereogram?

Whistling for Watson, I raced back up the beach, puffing and stumbling up the cliff steps. Reaching the bluff top I hastily clipped on Watson's leash, tucked Trixie under my arm, jay-jogged across the Pacific Coast Highway, and ran the half block back home.

. 15 .

Enter Tony

I FUMBLED THROUGH my bag for Debbie's telephone number, and hastily punched it in.

"Hello?"

"Hello, Debbie? It's Delilah Doolittle. We met yesterday when I took you home from the police station."

"Yes?" Was it my imagination or did she sound a little apprehensive?

"You mentioned a dog you and Steven were looking after for a friend. What kind of a dog was it?"

She hesitated. "Uh, it was one of those police dogs."

"You mean a German shepherd?"

"Yeah, I guess so. A German shepherd."

"What color, sex?"

"Kind of black and tan, male."

"Bingo!" I said, thinking aloud.

"That's not its name," she said.

"What? Oh, never mind, I was thinking of something else." For some reason—I was guessing now but it seemed like a good guess to me—Steven had taken Herbie. Debbie lived miles from Jessica. If it was Herbie who had run away from her, I had been looking for him in the wrong neighbourhood. Maybe I was jumping to conclusions—admittedly a failing of mine, you might say my favourite form of exercise—but this was just too much of a coincidence.

Not knowing whether or not Debbie knew that Herbie was stolen, I said no more. If she was involved in the dognapping scheme, I had already said too much. I covered as best I could by saying something about an Irish setter I knew of that had been found in that neighbourhood and I had wondered if it might have been her friend's dog, and I left it at that.

Why hadn't it occurred to me sooner that Steven might have taken Herbie? If I had picked up on it yesterday when Debbie told me about the friend's missing dog, I could have started looking for him straightaway. Instead I had lost valuable time entertaining Evie. The sooner I got back on the job the better. I would have to print up some more flyers to distribute in the Westgrove area.

I took a quick shower, changing from shorts and tee shirt into cotton khaki jeans and a jungle print blouse. I was reaching for my keys, and Watson was already on her feet, when I heard a car pull up outside. In the driveway was a classic woody station wagon, with a vintage long board sticking out the rear window, and bearing a vanity license plate which indicated the owner was a senior surfer. The driver, wearing black OP surfing shorts and a white tank tee shirt proclaiming "I survived the July 4th Surf City Pierfest," approached the back door. He looked remarkably fit and tanned for a man in his seventies. The lines around his eyes, reflecting years of squinting at the sun, deepened as he grinned, confident of a warm welcome.

"Tony," I greeted him at the door. "What in the world's going on? I heard the police picked you up in connection with the Steven Potter murder."

He leaned over to pick up Trixie, who was circling him in a paroxysm of joy.

"Yes, but they had to let me go, didn't they? They can only hold you for so long, then they either have to charge you with something or release you." He ran a gnarled hand over the few remaining grey hairs, sparse as a fledgling's down, on his tanned, balding pate, and went on. "When the Old Bill nabbed me this time, I said to meself, 'It's all up with you, Tony, old cock.' But here I am, turning up like the proverbial bad penny." His nonchalance didn't fool me in the least. While this certainly wasn't his first brush with the law, it wasn't for petty larceny this time.

He looked hopefully around the kitchen. "Any chance of a cuppa?"

"Of course," I said, plugging in the electric teakettle, which stood ready to offer comfort or stimulation, as required, at any time—morning, noon, or night or, as now, at eleven o'clock in the morning. "But however did you get involved?"

"They really stitched me up this time," he said. "Me prints was all over the dog'ouse, wasn't they? I 'elped Steve move it over to the paddock meself. Mrs. L. wanted it moved out of the dog run to the paddock to give the dogs more room while she was away. Turns out I was the last one to see him alive. But I didn't do him in, s'welp me God, I didn't." He shuddered, no doubt recalling the gruesome manner in which poor Steven had met his end. "Someone else done it, and now they're trying to make me carry the can back."

Really, the man talked like he'd just got off the boat, instead of having lived here for forty years or more.

"But why were you at Jessica Lomax's in the first place?" I asked.

He was surprised that I knew so much about the murder, and I filled him in on my involvement while I made and poured his tea.

"Sugar?" I asked. Milk was a given among the Brits of my acquaintance. He nodded and I asked him again, "What were you doing there?"

"Ta, luv," he said, taking the cup and saucer and pulling up a seat at the kitchen table. "Steve owed me money. I knew he was working for Ratchett, so I called over there.

Ratchett told me I could find him at Mrs. Lomax's. Of course, Steve didn't have the money. All gone up his nose, I expect.'' He shrugged, took a gulp of tea, smacked his lips, proclaimed, ''Lovely cup of char,'' then continued. ''He told me he was onto some scam where he'd be able to pay me back big-time.''

''Did he give you any idea what he was up to?'' I asked.

''No. Only that he would be able to pay me back in a few days.''

''Did you tell the police about the scam?'' I persisted. ''It might be a clue to the murder.''

''What's to tell? I had no idea what he had going. Didn't want to know. But I should've known better than to lend him money. Druggies . . .''

''You don't . . . ?'' I hesitated.

''Do drugs? Nah, that's a mug's game.'' He paused to pour tea into my best bone china saucer. ''Police think I killed him because he wouldn't pay me back.'' He leaned down and placed the saucer on the floor. Trixie lapped at it eagerly.

I told him of my meeting with Debbie and my suspicions that the dog she was supposed to have been watching might be the missing Herbie. Was it possible that Steven took the dog, intending to ransom him to Jessica?

''Could be,'' Tony said, nodding. ''That's just the type of thing he'd be capable of, anything for a quick buck.''

''But that's so cruel,'' I said, and went on to tell him of my visit to Jim Ratchett's. ''Do you think he could have killed Steven?''

''Nah, he's a nasty piece of work, and that's a dodgy operation he's got going there with the sentry dog business an' all, but I can't see him doing his own nevvie. And what's to be gained by it?''

''Perhaps there's a family inheritance involved,'' I hazarded. ''Something we don't know about. At any rate, I'm convinced that whoever did it has something to do with what happened here last night.''

I told him about the break-in and the warning note I had received, and the refusal of the police to make any connection between Herbie's disappearance and the murder.

"That Detective Mallory is the most irritating man," I complained. "He refuses to consider the possibility that a valuable dog like Herbie could provide a motive for murder."

"Oh, Mallory's a decent enough bloke, for a copper," said Tony. "Just not got much imagination. And you have to admit, your theory's a bit far-fetched."

I was not prepared to admit any such thing.

" 'Ow much do I owe you for Trixie's bail, then?" he asked. I gave him the shelter impound fee receipt, and he repaid me from a wad of grubby fifty and twenty dollar bills that he pulled from his pocket, saying as he placed them on the kitchen counter, "They're a bit scruffy, but as my old dad used to say, 'There's no such thing as dirty money.' " He chuckled.

I wasn't so sure his old dad was right, and wondered how Tony had come by so much cash. Talk about dodgy operations. But he was no murderer, of that I was sure. Undeniably he moved in a dubious milieu, but he would never knowingly hurt anyone. Now I had yet another reason for solving this case—to help clear Tony. He really was a dear, for all that right now he was being a bit of a hindrance.

I was anxious to get on over to Debbie's, but as Tony showed no signs of leaving, I left him and Trixie to the teapot, and went to work in my den-cum-office to see what I could accomplish from home.

I scanned the lost and found columns to make sure my ad for Herbie was in—it was—and to see if there were any found German shepherds—there weren't. Then I called Rita at the shelter to ask her if any more German shepherds had been impounded. No luck there either. It was a slow week for German shepherds.

Next I pulled out the yellow pages and called animal

hospitals in the Westgrove area to inquire if Herbie might have been taken in injured. The third call got me excited.

"Yes, we did have a German shepherd brought in hit by a car a couple of nights ago," said the receptionist at the Westgrove Small Animal Emergency Clinic. "I think it's still here. Just a minute, I'll check."

I waited anxiously. If it was Herbie, my problems were over. Get over there, pick up the dog, return it to Jessica, and be done with the whole tiresome business.

"Yes," said the receptionist, returning to the phone. "It's a German shepherd, black and tan."

"Any ID?" I said.

"Just a flea collar is all," she replied. Flea collar? That didn't sound right. One more question.

"Male or female?"

In the couple of minutes it took her to go back and check once more I had mentally collected my fee, made the mortgage payment, and was enjoying a well-earned day off. Her voice jolted me back to reality. "Female," she said.

"Female? You're sure?" What was the matter with me? Of course she was sure. "Forgive me," I said lamely. "I'm looking for a male. I was so hoping this was it."

Disappointed, I debated what to do next. Should I call Jessica and give her a progress report, tell her that Herbie was last seen in the Westgrove area? But how sure was I of that? It was only a hunch that the dog Debbie had been harbouring was Herbie. I didn't want to give out false hope. Also, if I told Jessica that much, I'd also have to tell her of my suspicions about Steven's taking the dog, and about Tony. It was all too complicated to explain. I had just decided that call could wait, when the phone rang. It was Jessica herself. Did I have anything to report? I confined my response to a simple "possible sighting" in the Westgrove area.

"I would remind you again, Mrs. Doolittle, that I want Herbie found before he is picked up by the authorities. I do not want him going to the animal shelter. I cannot emphasize this enough.''

Why, I wondered, do people have such a dread of animal shelters? A lost pet is always better off there than roaming the streets hungry and scared. It may be the end of the line for an unfortunate few, but for many it is the place of happy reunions with their owners, or of being adopted by new families.

''There is a thousand-dollar bonus in it for you, if you find him before he gets to the pound,'' Jessica was saying.

Well, that got my attention. But it also aroused my curiosity. Why was it so important that Herbie not go to the shelter? He was sure to have had all his shots; and if he picked up a few fleas, well, a shampoo and flea dip would soon take care of that.

I told her I would do my best, and promised to call her the minute I had anything new to report. I hoped I sounded more positive than I felt. For it had just occurred to me that perhaps Debbie hadn't been telling me the truth. Maybe Herbie had not run away but had been passed along to an accomplice. Ratchett, possibly? Or how about the friend who had taken Steven to Debbie's that night? What about the roommate? What indeed. I wondered if Tony knew anything about those two. As soon as I finished up here I would ask him.

I considered calling Detective Mallory to tell him my suspicions about Steven taking Herbie, but thought better of it. He refused to see any connection between the murder and the missing dog, and in order to convince him, I would have to betray Tony's confidence, and it might make things worse for him. Though he had been released, he was still considered a suspect. Anyway, Mallory would surely once again admonish me to stay out of police business.

I checked my notes to make sure there were no calls I'd neglected to return. Mrs. Jones' was still outstanding, but I decided to delay calling her for a while longer. Bad news could always keep, and there was still a chance that her poodle might show up before the end of the day.

There was one more call I had to make that morning. I wanted to find out more about electronic collars, how effective they were, and how much damage they could inflict if handled improperly. In particular, was it possible they could harm a human? Going through my mental Rolodex for who might have that kind of information, I came up with Pam Harvey, a local dog trainer. I dialled her number and left a message on her machine asking her to call me as soon as it was convenient.

My hand was still on the phone when it rang again. I picked it up. ''Delilah Doolittle,'' I answered.

A woman was crying. ''Thank God you're home,'' she said.

· 16 ·

Lost, Stolen, or Mislaid

"THANK GOD I didn't get that blasted machine." She sounded close to hysteria.

"Evie? Is that you? What in the world's the matter?" She couldn't have been home very long. Was she calling to apologize for her outburst earlier this morning? But that was no call for tears.

"Chamois is gone!" She choked on the words.

"Gone! What do you mean, gone?" I asked stupidly, taken by surprise.

"Lost. Stolen. I don't know," she sobbed. "I arrived home about half an hour ago. When I reached over to the backseat for his carryall, it wasn't there. If anything happens to that dog, I'll just die."

For Evie to have somehow mislaid Chamois seemed more than a trifle careless. However this was no time for a lecture.

She had apparently been so absorbed with the new car that she had scarcely given a thought to Chamois on the drive home, and had not once bothered to check if all her baggage was on board.

"I wondered if I had left him in your car," she said between sobs.

I remembered checking the back of my car to make sure she hadn't forgotten anything when I dropped her off at the Mercedes dealer. I knew she had left nothing behind.

"No. I'm sorry. Did you stop anywhere on the way home?"

"I stopped for petrol in San Clemente and went to the restroom. Oh, and at the corner market just before I got home. I needed ciggies," she added lamely.

Good Lord, the dog could be anywhere.

"He has never left the house without one of us. He will be so scared on his own," Evie continued between sobs.

I didn't doubt it. My heart ached for both of them. "Now listen to me," I said firmly. "Do you recall seeing the carrier in the car when you stopped in San Clemente?"

"Hang on a minute," she said. "Howard's trying to say something." I heard muffled conversation. Then Evie came back on the line.

"If this is your idea of a joke, Dee, I don't think much of your sense of humour."

"Whatever do you mean?"

"We just received a, a . . ." She was too distraught to go on.

"Let me speak to Howard," I said firmly.

"Hallo, Delilah." It was a relief to hear Howard's calm, kindly voice after Evie's hysteria. "What Evie's trying to tell you is that we've just received a faxed message threatening our dog. She says it's similar to the one she found at your house yesterday."

"Read it to me, Howard."

"It says: 'If you want to see your dog again, get Doolittle off the Lomax case,'" Howard's deep Texas drawl intoned. "What's going on, Delilah?"

"That's what I'd like to know." I was beginning to feel out of my depth, threatened by invisible forces, and faced with the gradual realization that we were dealing with someone whose desperation to keep me from finding Herbie was driving him to extreme lengths. If it was the murderer, he was getting too close to my friends for comfort. I had been inclined to dismiss the first note as a minor distraction to my search, but now I realized I would have to take the whole thing much more seriously.

Who would know of Evie's whereabouts and about her dog? Someone must have overheard a mention of Chamois when she was here yesterday. But who, and how could they have acted so quickly? Or was it a chance opportunity that he had recklessly seized upon without a preconceived plan? The questions came fast, the answers not at all. The stakes must be a lot higher than I had at first thought. There was more to this case than a runaway dog and the killing of a shiftless drug addict.

"Another thing," Howard was saying. "How would these people know our telephone number?"

At last a question I could answer. "They would have got that from Chamois' ID tag, or maybe there was a tag on his carrier," I replied.

Evie came back on the line, inconsolable.

"My poor baby," she wailed. "How do I know he's being taken care of? He gets so depressed if he doesn't take his Prozac."

Ye gods, what next, liposuction? No wonder the little lad looked so bemused all the time. Though I knew some vets prescribed the antidepressant to treat separation anxiety, I held firmly to the opinion that mood-altering drugs had no place in a pet's medicine cabinet, and that the best treatment for such pet conditions was plenty of exercise and companionship, remedies that wouldn't do their owners any harm either.

"This is what comes of you getting mixed up with unsavoury people, Dee," Evie was saying. "If you're so damned clever at finding other people's lost pets, you'd better get yourself down here and find Chamois. It's all your fault."

She didn't have to remind me. Somehow or another my best friend had become involved in my investigation. Finding Chamois would have to be my priority now.

"Please calm down. Try not to worry. I promise you we'll find him." Find him! I couldn't even find Herbie, here on my own turf, let alone a dog lost somewhere between here and San Diego. I'd been looking for Herbie for three days now, and I was no closer to finding him than when Jessica had first called. And yet. Maybe I was getting close. I was obviously getting up somebody's nose, to judge by how hard they were trying to get me to quit.

"I'll be there by mid-afternoon," I promised.

The tears abated now she had my promise, but I was not forgiven. "Get it sorted out, Dee, and quickly. Howard has already called the police."

I doubted that the police in San Diego would get any more excited about a missing dog than they did in Surf City, as my own recent experiences had proved.

I wasn't even sure what good I could do in San Diego. The key to the matter was here, with Herbie, and it was becoming increasingly clear that Jessica hadn't told me everything. I intended to confront her about that at the first opportunity, but that satisfaction would have to be delayed until my return from San Diego. Evie needed my support. She would never forgive me if I didn't make some effort to start the search from there.

How to get there was the next problem. My car had to go into the shop again before I took a trip of any distance. It certainly wasn't up to the 100-mile drive to San Diego. Evie's train journey of yesterday had seemed straightforward enough. The schedule I had picked up at the station when I met her was still in my purse. Why not?

A quick call confirmed that there was a train leaving for San Diego within the hour. I could just make it.

I returned to the kitchen to find Tony and Trixie munching on the imported English crumpets I had stashed away in the freezer for a time when I was feeling especially homesick and in need of comfort food. Tony wiped buttery fingers down his tee shirt, while Trixie licked her chops for the last crumb. I stifled my protest. I had a favour to ask.

"Look," I said. "I have to go to San Diego on an emergency." I filled him in on what had happened. "I don't trust my car to make the trip so I'm going by train and will stay overnight. Dogs aren't allowed on the train. Will you keep an eye on Watson while I'm gone?"

Tony readily agreed, and while I changed yet again (into a dress and heels this time) and tossed a few things into an overnight bag, he went around the house checking windows and doors against another break-in. The futility of this effort became only too apparent when he came across the broken window. Preoccupied with Evie and everything else that had happened yesterday, I had completely forgotten to call someone to get it fixed.

"Don't worry about it, luv," said Tony. "I'll have a mate of mine pop round and take care of it this afternoon. If nothing else, we'll get it boarded up for you for the time being."

The doggie door, too, had to remain unbolted, in order to give Watson free access to the backyard, though I knew she would probably opt to stay in the house most of the time. Tony promised to check on her several times during my absence, and I hoped that his visits would provide sufficient distraction from any carpet-chewing she might contemplate. And I expected to be back by this time tomorrow.

Leaving a doleful Watson on guard duty, we left the house at the same time, Tony and Trixie to head home to their trailer, I to the station where less than twenty-four hours earlier I had met Evie. I left my car in the overnight parking section, grabbed my holdall and knitting bag, and made the 1:15 departure with about five minutes to spare.

. 17 .

Strangers on a Train

THERE WERE NOT many people travelling at this time of day, and I had my choice of seats. The only other occupants of my coach were a young mother with two flaxen-haired little girls of about six and four years old. Probably off to visit the San Diego Zoo or Sea World, I guessed.

Selecting a window seat, I picked up my knitting and settled down to enjoy a leisurely ride. I was making an afghan for Watson's chair, to cover the rips she had made with her heavy claws. Afghans for my friends' pets, and cosies for their teapots, are about all I ever aspire to these days. Both are simple to make and don't need a lot of concentration. I cannot abide complete idleness, and find knitting to be very relaxing.

Just as the train was about to pull out, there was a flurry of activity, and a man wearing a dark grey business suit and carrying a newspaper and a folded raincoat hurried aboard, taking a seat across the aisle, facing me.

''Just made it,'' he said with an embarrassed laugh. Not wishing to invite conversation, I gave a barely nodded acknowledgment and returned to my knitting.

It was a long time since I'd been on a train, not since I used to go down to England's west country to stay with

Evie during the school holidays. If I needed to look for a reason for abandoning my client and rushing to Evie's side, I had only to think back to those days, when she had earned my eternal, though never unquestioning, loyalty. Even then she had been my friend and protector, the latter a role she still tried to assume at every possible excuse today, witness her verbal assault on poor Officer Offley.

The first part of the journey offered little to delight the eye. Row upon row of houses terraced into hillsides crept like some contagious disease, scarring forever the natural beauty of the region. But gradually the painful reminders of overdevelopment were left behind, and I laid aside my knitting to enjoy the passing scene. Cool lagoons and broad ocean vistas, pelicans and fishing boats rolled by as we rattled on through communities with romantic-sounding Spanish names—San Juan Capistrano, San Clemente—reminding one of California's colourful past.

After a while I became aware that the man across the aisle was watching me from behind his newspaper. It seemed that every time I glanced in his direction I would catch his eye. Drat the man. I hoped he wasn't going to try to engage me in conversation. I didn't flatter myself that he was smitten with me, though I was wearing one of my smarter outfits—a floral two-piece dress and jacket, with a good label which, in a weak moment, I had allowed Evie to talk me into buying from a consignment shop.

No. My nerves, on edge from the events of the past few days, led me to suspect the man of something far more sinister. Was he following me? Why was he carrying a raincoat on one of the hottest days of the year? Was it to hide a gun? I stole a closer look. Middle-aged, medium build, sandy hair, gold-rimmed spectacles, he looked harmless enough. The perfect hit man, in fact. He'd blend into a crowd and no one would ever remember seeing him.

You're letting your imagination run away with you, I chided myself. But I couldn't shake the feeling of uneasiness. I was comforted by the presence of the little family at the far end of the coach, now absorbed in playing with Barbie dolls. Surely the man wouldn't try anything with witnesses present?

That reassurance was short-lived. When we pulled into Oceanside, the mother and children, in a clatter of excitement, tumbled off the train and into the welcoming embrace of a young Marine corporal, no doubt from nearby Camp Pendleton. So assiduously had I been avoiding eye contact with the stranger that I had missed their preparations to alight.

I could have got up and moved down the train, but I refused to give in to my fears. I put away my knitting, keeping out one of the needles, the closest thing to a weapon I possessed. And the next time the man glanced my way, I fixed him with a glare calculated to freeze further advances.

I felt relieved, and not a little silly, when the train finally pulled into San Diego without further incident. Even so, I let the man alight first and allowed him to get well ahead of me before leaving the train myself. I followed him down the platform at a safe distance, then lost sight of him after we entered the vast Santa Fe concourse which, with its high vaulted ceilings, put me in mind of the great London terminals—Waterloo, Victoria, Paddington—I grew up with. If it hadn't been for the lamentable purpose of my visit I might have lingered awhile to soak up the atmosphere. As it was, I reluctantly dragged my attention back to the business at hand.

It was with that business in mind that, on an impulse, instead of taking a taxi immediately to Evie's as I had intended, I crossed the Santa Fe courtyard and hopped onto a trolley-car which was about to depart. There was someone I wanted to talk to first.

ABSORBED IN JUGGLING holdall and knitting bag as I groped through my purse for the right change, I gave no attention to the other passengers on the trolley. It was with considerable consternation therefore, that, having paid my fare and made my way to the first available seat, I found I had plopped myself down next to the stranger with the rain-coat.

· 18 ·
Tea Tattle

"GOING TO THE border?" he asked, amiably enough.

My goodness. I hoped he didn't think that *I* was following *him*.

"No. Just a couple of stops," I replied frostily, throwing in for good measure, "My husband is meeting me." I was determined to cut short any further attempt at conversation. Though it was now quite obvious that, unless he was a mind reader and knew even before I did that I was going to catch the trolley, he could not possibly have any sinister intentions.

I got off the trolley at Market Street and walked the rest of the way to my destination, a small wood frame house in an old section of town. Flowers dominated the tiny front yard. Overgrown bougainvillaea, leggy geraniums, and full-blown roses, a little past their prime in the September heat. A neatly painted wooden sign announced "ST. DAVID'S WELSH CORGIS AND GROOMING."

I pushed open the gate and climbed the steps to the porch. My arrival had set off the dogs, and I had to knock several times on the screen door to be heard over the noise. Finally, a shout of "Quiet, or it's off to the sausage factory with the lot of ye,'' had the desired effect, and the barking subsided.

Molly Rhys-Davies came to the door, a half-shaved black-and-white Shih Tzu under one arm.

''Indeed to goodness, look you,'' she said. Her lilting Welsh accent hadn't diminished one bit after thirty years in the United States. Her greying black hair, straight as a yard of pump water, was cut in what we used to call a pudding basin bob. Her short dumpy figure was encased in faded black sweats, covered in dog hair.

Molly was part of a loose-knit circle of expatriate Brits in southern California, and our mutual interest in dogs had furthered the acquaintance. The grooming business kept her busy, and I had been fairly sure I'd find her home.

Molly raises Welsh Corgis. She could sell many more puppies than she actually does, particularly among her fellow Brits with whom the breed has a certain cachet as a favourite of the Royal Family, but she limits her production to one litter a year. Personally, I can't tell a Pembroke from a Cardigan, but I knew that Molly had a reputation for sound puppies with excellent temperament.

More to the point, she knew Jessica Lomax, and I was hoping she might be able to give me a little more insight into my client's character.

''Sit ye down. I'll make us a nice cup of tea soon as I'm done here. Nearly finished.'' She looped the Shih Tzu onto the grooming table and continued her work.

Molly was a competent groomer, but she was left-handed and appeared awkward as she wielded the clippers. Not someone I'd like near my private parts with a pair of shears, I thought, sympathizing with the fidgety Shih Tzu.

With a ''There, you'll do,'' Molly picked up the dog and moved over to a tub and commenced bathing him.

''What brings you to my doorstep?'' she said, raising her voice to be heard over the noise of the running water and the blow-dryers which were attached to elevated wire cages wherein sat several unhappy-looking dogs in various stages of grooming.

Molly loved to gossip. I knew that if she had anything worth knowing she would be happy to share it with me. But I would have to watch my tongue. I didn't want it getting back to Jessica that I had been snooping on her.

Through the Dutch door which gave into the backyard I could see Molly's two champion Corgis, Taffy and Daffodil, dozing in the sun. They gave me an idea.

I told her I might know of a good home for an orphan Corgi. Like many responsible breeders, Molly kept an eye out for her breed at the shelters and attempted to find them new homes.

"I'll keep you in mind," she said. "You know I ask for a donation toward the vet bill. Always get them fixed before I place them," she added. "Don't want them ending up in the wrong hands."

"What do you mean, 'wrong hands'?" I asked.

Molly put the Shih Tzu into a drying cage, then heated the teakettle on a hot plate.

"People get hold of a purebred dog and think they can make a few dollars doing some backyard breeding. No idea of the pedigree, or bloodlines," she said.

"But they wouldn't be able to show?"

"Oh, don't you be so sure, look you," she said, nodding her head knowingly. "Easy enough to make up false papers. Just use the pedigree of a similar dead animal. Or, when you register a litter of puppies, just add a couple more than the actual number, and you're all set. Paper hanging, that's what they call it. I tell you, in my opinion a breeder's reputation is your only guarantee of a dog's pedigree."

We talked in this vein for a few minutes longer until I was finally able to bring the conversation around to Jessica.

"I have a new client. I think you know her. Jessica Lomax? She's lost her German shepherd Herbie."

"Lost her champion?" Molly exclaimed. "What a pity. Not that I like the woman, but to lose her dog, that's a real shame. She has such high hopes for him, too. Thinks he's going to win best of breed at Westminster next year. But you'll find him, if anyone can,'' she added.

"I hope so,'' I said. ''But why do you dislike her?''

"Well, maybe dislike's too strong a word. She's a great judge, and she knows German shepherds better than anyone in the state, maybe the country. But she can get a bit stroppy at times.''

I smiled. I hadn't heard that expression for a long time. "So she can be opinionated, strong-willed, perhaps. But that's not unusual in a show judge, surely?''

Molly nodded, then went on. ''But it's the way she talks to people. And show-off!'' She rolled her eyes. ''Swanning around the show ring like Lady Muck in those long skirts of hers, look you.'' She set out two mugs on a tea tray, then continued, ''Did you know she used to work at the pound?''

This was a surprise. ''She did?'' I exclaimed.

"Yes. At the shelter near you. Actually, she was working in the clinic as an intern while she studied to be a vet tech. But she moved on soon after she got her certificate. Found it too depressing seeing animals put to sleep.''

"Well, can't say that I blame her,'' I said.

"That vet tech training is really useful for anyone working with dogs, like we do. You can give your own shots, for a start. Helpful at whelping time, too. And Jessica'll do anything for those dogs of hers. Devoted to 'em.'' Molly went on, warming to her subject. ''I hear she's willed everything to them. And she wants her ashes scattered over Madison Square Garden during the Westminster Dog Show. Did you ever hear the like?''

I had to confess I never had.

She poured the tea.

"Did you speak to her at the show last week?'' I asked casually.

"Not really. I'd wanted to ask her about getting a shepherd puppy for a friend of mine, but she didn't seem inclined to chat."

"How so?" I picked a dog hair out of my tea.

"Distracted. I thought I'd catch her later at the best of group dinner, but she didn't show up. Didn't even come out of her trailer the whole evening. I heard she was sick."

The trailer. She must be referring to the Winnebago I had seen in Jessica's driveway the other day.

"She must have been poorly to miss out on an opportunity to queen it over the rest of us," Molly continued. "Loves to be the center of attention, that one, all the breeders fawning over her."

A pity Jessica had to miss what was obviously an important event to her. "What day was that?" I asked.

"There's a program there, under the appointment book." Molly nodded in the direction of a cluttered desk.

The show schedule indicated that Jessica had judged the German shepherds on Tuesday morning, the herding group (where the best German shepherd, Corgi, Collie, Sheltie, and others competed for best of the herding-type dogs) on Wednesday afternoon, and the grand finale, the best in show, on Saturday evening. The dinner honouring the herding group was held on Wednesday.

Feeling that I had wormed all I could out of Molly without arousing her suspicions, I soon after made my exit, thanking her for the tea and promising to stay in touch.

I walked the short distance to the business district to hail a taxi, keeping a sharp lookout for my hit man as I went. Groundless as my fears probably were, I was still jumpy and couldn't shake the feeling I was being followed. Don't be ridiculous, I told myself. Probably the poor man is in the bosom of his family by now, completely unaware of the bag of nerves to which he has reduced the disagreeable woman he met on the train.

The pleasant taxi ride through Balboa Park to Evie's place was all too short. I was not looking forward in the least to the scene awaiting my arrival.

· 19 ·

Talking To Howard

"SHE'LL NEVER GET over it if we don't find the little rascal." Howard helped himself to another generous serving of sausages and tomatoes from the sideboard.

"Not to worry," I said, with my customary morning optimism. "We'll find him. Would you pass the HP sauce, please?"

Rosa, Evie's longtime cook and housekeeper, though originally from Mexico, had, through trial and error, mastered the mysteries of English cuisine, and breakfast at Evie's was always an event. Though I may not be the best judge of such things. Other people's food is invariably better than mine.

"Howard married me for my English breakfast," Evie liked to joke.

The Cavendish sideboard did indeed groan. The tantalizing aromas of kippers, grilled mushrooms and tomatoes, bacon, fried bread, and kidneys wafted from beneath the lids of silver servers. Thick slices of buttery toast awaited anointing by imported preserves—Dundee marmalade, English blackberry and apple jam.

Howard and Evie were Jack Sprat and his wife personified. Howard, tall and lean, never gained an ounce, while poor Evie only had to look at a lettuce leaf to put on five pounds. But for Evie food was a sensuous experience, and she derived as much enjoyment from feeding others as she did herself. She loved to entertain, and their two-story condo overlooking the golf course was the perfect setting for her parties and little dinners.

Rising early, I had found Howard already at breakfast, leafing through the latest issue of *Field & Stream*.

Howard is a "closet" hunter. That is to say he used to enjoy hunting and fishing before Evie "straightened him out," as she says. Devoted to her, he deserves more credit than she, I'm sure, that their marriage has lasted over thirty years. Tall, sparsely grey, with the kindliest face, he was now in his early sixties. He was a self-made man whose fortune had burgeoned along with southern California development in the seventies and eighties.

I had arrived the previous afternoon to find Evie totally overwrought.

"Please try to think," I begged her. "When do you last remember seeing Chamois?"

"Maybe, I don't know . . . Maybe at the car showroom. I took my bags out of your car, I remember Chamois was in his carryall, and put them, put them . . ."

"Yes," I encouraged.

"Put them on the sidewalk while we waited for the Mercedes to be brought round. Oh—my—God. . . ."

She put her hands to her face. "I don't remember putting him in the car," she cried with horror.

"But surely . . ." I broke off. It was useless to speculate. But I had stood on the sidewalk and watched her leave. Surely I would have noticed if she'd left anything behind.

Evie had finally been persuaded to go to bed with a sedative. I could have used one myself. I had spent a restless night in the luxurious guest room, Evie's reproaches echoing in my ears.

There was nothing useful I could do here. I had done all I could. I advised them to put up signs in the neighbourhood, and to check the shelter every day, just in case Chamois had been stolen locally and had managed to escape the clutches of his kidnapper. I really didn't think that very likely, but it gave them something positive to do. We also placed ads in the lost and found columns of all the southern California editions of the *Los Angeles Times*, offering a reward for Chamois' safe return.

"If he's being held for ransom, this should produce results," I said. "Or it may bring someone forward who saw something." Though I did have my doubts. The fax had indicated that Chamois' kidnapping had something to do with my case, and I didn't think ransom was the motive. Perhaps Detective Mallory would be able to trace the fax. Though it had probably been sent from a print shop. I doubted anyone would be foolish enough to use their own fax machine.

I had made the trip down here more to give solace and comfort than with any expectation of finding the dog, and I really felt my time would be better spent back in Surf City looking for Herbie who, I prayed, would lead me to Chamois.

As I was now explaining to Howard. Evie was still in bed, the sedative having finally taken effect about 2 a.m. I had followed him into the kitchen, where he was preparing a tea tray to take up to her room. The elegant teapot, I was pleased to see, was covered with one of my own knitted tea cosies.

"You're right," he said. "Why don't I take you to the station before Evie wakes up? I'll explain it to her after you've left."

I was grateful. I had not relished the thought of trying to explain to Evie why I was abandoning her in her hour of need. To her way of thinking I should be here, hand holding. She would be furious when she realized I was gone, but I told myself all would be forgiven once I was able to return Chamois to her.

As Howard opened the front door to escort me out, we

came face-to-face with a man standing with his hand poised to press the doorbell. Though tennis clothes had replaced the business suit, he was unmistakably my hit man from yesterday.

"Ted!" exclaimed Howard, slapping the heel of his hand against his forehead. "I'm sorry. In all the upset I completely forgot about our game." He started to explain about Chamois, then seeing Ted glance inquiringly in my direction, recovered his manners and said, "Oh, sorry. I thought you two knew each other. Ted Willoughby, this is Evie's friend, Delilah Doolittle. We're just off to the station. She's on her way back to Surf City."

Ted, reaching out to shake my hand, said, "Of course! I knew I'd met you somewhere before. That's why I kept staring at you yesterday. It was here at a Christmas party a couple of years ago."

Well, if he said so. I had absolutely no recollection of ever having met him before.

Now it was Howard's turn to look puzzled. Ted and I both started to explain at once; then, as we all made our way to the lift and down to the underground parking area, I stopped talking and let Ted relate the encounter. He made much less of my rudeness than he might have, I thought. Though I did detect just the slightest hint of malice in his, "And how is your husband?"

Duly chastened, I huddled in embarrassed silence in the comfort of Howard's Jaguar while the two men rescheduled their tennis game. It is well to know when to lie low.

HOWARD DELIVERED ME to the station in time to catch the ten-thirty train, and I was back in Surf City well before one p.m.

I picked up my car and hurried home, anxious to see Watson. At this time of the day she would doubtless be dozing in the shade of her favourite tree in the backyard, though the sound of my car would bring her to her feet, and to the side gate, which faced the driveway.

"Hi, baby, Mummy's home." I was a little surprised when her slightly overweight form did not come wriggling excitedly toward me down the garden path. She must be indoors. Hurriedly unlocking the back door, I called again.

"Watson?" My greeting echoed through the empty house.

Watson was gone.

· 20 ·

Going to the Dogs

I DID A thorough check of the premises, inside and out, but the panic that had set in the minute Watson didn't come when I called the first time proved to be justified. There was no way she would not be alert to the arrival of a car, to the opening of the gate, to the sound of my voice.

Had she run off to pay me back for leaving her behind? Not likely. Though she had a mind of her own and her feelings were easily hurt, she was too smart and too fond of her creature comforts to chance life in the unknown. Maybe Tony had taken her for a walk. I raced to the kitchen phone to call him. But before I reached it, I saw the note. Attached to the tea cosy with a clothes-peg, it was brief and to the point: *"Third and final notice. If you want your dog back, quit looking for Herbie."*

Fear and guilt vied for dominance in my emotions. I should never have gone to San Diego, should never have left Watson behind. In three days I had not been able to come up with a single trace of Herbie, and now I had lost Watson and Chamois into the bargain.

Who would gain by my giving up the search? If Debbie knew that Steven had kidnapped Herbie, she might well not want me to find out. But what difference would it make to her now that Steven was dead? Anyway, I doubted she had the nerve, and she certainly didn't have the transportation, needed to pull off a stunt like this.

Watson would never have gone willingly. It would take expertise to lure her away from home. Whoever had taken her would have to have a knowledge of dog behaviour, as well as equipment or some sort of enticement.

Everything pointed to Jim Ratchett. I was convinced that both the solution to the murder and the missing dogs were to be found at his compound.

Surely when confronted with this note and the account of Chamois' kidnapping, Detective Mallory would have to acknowledge that Herbie's disappearance might have something to do with Steven Potter's murder. I couldn't wait to tell him. But when I telephoned his office, Officer Offley told me he was out. I didn't want Mallory to get the information secondhand. And with his attitude I didn't trust Offley not to downplay the significance of my message, so I simply left word to the effect that I was onto something at Jim Ratchett's place and that I was headed there now.

I would have to change before I left. In deference to Evie's notions of appropriate attire for all occasions, I had worn the floral two-piece and strappy white heels for the trip to San Diego. I needed something more comfortable for the coming confrontation with Jim Ratchett. I hastily changed into tan jeans, a matching tan and white checked shirt, and my desert boots. Just as I was fastening the last shirt button, I noticed that it was hanging by a thread. Blast. No time for "saving nine" now. I wound the thread around the remaining fast stitches and hoped for the best.

I called Tony and left a message on his machine letting him know I was back, and asking him to keep a lookout for Watson in case she should somehow manage to come home on her own. Then with a heavy heart I set out to find my dog.

It was late afternoon by the time I pulled into Ratchett's parking lot. His beat-up old truck was there. Good. I was afraid I might have missed him. At this time of the day he could have been out delivering his guard dogs to the various used-car lots and industrial sites that rented them for night duty. Without Steven, he was sure to be shorthanded.

It was quiet. No dogs were being worked in the training area, and I was thankful to be spared a repeat of the scene with the Brittanys from the other day. The only noise came from the freeway traffic and the occasional bark of the dogs penned up in the back.

I walked over to the trailer office and peered through the screen door. Ratchett was taking a nap in his executive swivel chair. The chair's back was toward me, but I could see his jeans-clad legs stretched out on the metal desk, his feet resting on top of a scattering of business papers. The day's sports events were being reported on a portable television which sat on metal utility shelving on the other side of the room, opposite the door. He must have dozed off while watching the news. A couple of Coors bottles sweated condensation marks onto the desk.

I decided I would check the dogs in the kennel before confronting him. If Watson and Chamois were there, I would just release them and go. Not much chance of finding Herbie there. If my guess was correct and the dog Debbie had been minding was in fact Herbie, he was more likely to be picked up by animal control at this point.

As soon as I stepped into the kennel area the barking started. I didn't care. My dander was really up now. How dare this man go round stealing people's dogs! And then sit there drinking beer and watching television without a thought to the anguish he was causing. If the noise brought him out of his office, so much the better. I'd demand that Chamois and Watson be released. If he threatened me, I would tell him the police were on their way.

The kennels housed a dozen or so miserable-looking junkyard dogs—mostly mixes of shepherds, Rotties, Dobies, and who-knew-what. No sign of Watson or Chamois, though two of the cages were empty. Had they been there earlier and been spirited away before my arrival? Sensing a friend, most of the dogs ceased barking and started whining pathetically when they saw me.

Their food and water bowls were empty. Something else to take up with Mr. Ratchett. I marched back to the trailer, steeling myself for what was bound to be an unpleasant confrontation. I tapped on the screen door.

"Mr. Ratchett," I called. No reply. He was still asleep. I knocked again. The screen door was off the latch so I pushed it open and walked over to him, skirting the chair to where I could see his face, intending to nudge him gently awake.

No use. Jim Ratchett had tormented his last dog.

After the initial wave of horror and nausea, my first reaction was to get out of there fast. He had not been dead long; if I averted my eyes from his distorted face, bulging above the choking electronic collar, I could fancy he was still dozing. There were none of the flies or the sickening odour that had attended my discovery of the wretched body in the doghouse.

I found myself outside the trailer gasping for air, my mind reeling with questions. Who killed him? If he didn't kill Steven, then who did? My theory on the case had as many holes as Swiss cheese. Once again I had jumped to the wrong conclusion. My client, my best friend, and now my own precious dog were all victims of my impatience and tendency to draw assumptions from too little information.

I was about to go back inside the office to dial 911 when I hesitated. I had already left a message for Mallory, telling him of my intentions; he should be here at any moment. I was becoming uncomfortably aware that I might be regarded as a prime suspect. Finding one dead body could happen to anyone. Two in one week might well be considered one too many. Clearly I had more at stake in solving this crime than anyone.

Now was no time to be fainthearted. Plucking up my

courage I went back into the office to look for clues. Clues? I wasn't a policeman. I wouldn't know a clue if it jumped up and bit me. For what, exactly, would I be looking? On the desk a portable fan gently riffled a pile of what looked to be invoices and bank statements, together with a check register. Ratchett must have been in the act of balancing his checkbook when he was killed. I wondered how much he made at this junkyard dog racket. Carefully avoiding looking at his face, I took a pencil from the desk and gingerly reached over the body to draw the register toward me.

It looked like a lucrative business. One item in particular piqued my interest. In addition to the deposits from businesses for guard dog rental, and clients for field training, there was a regular monthly deposit of one thousand dollars, with only an indecipherable initial for the payor.

The tile floor felt gritty under my feet. It obviously hadn't seen a mop for months, if ever. My foot hit something small and hard. There goes my shirt button, I thought. I reached down and, groping in the dark under the desk, found it and slipped it into my jeans pocket.

The sun was about to set and the light was getting dim. Concerned about fingerprints, I had refrained from turning on a light, and in the creeping shadows, with the only sounds the murmuring fan and the inanities of a television game show, I had the uneasy feeling that I was being watched. Could the murderer still be on the premises? There had been no other car in the parking lot.

I wanted to leave, but I wasn't sure it was correct procedure to leave the scene of the crime. I wished Detective Mallory would get here. Where was he anyway? Perhaps he didn't get my message. Officer Offley had not sounded very interested. Maybe Mallory just didn't think it important. *Mrs. Doolittle still waffling on about dogs, is she?* Should I call him again? But there was no way I could reach the phone without having to look at Ratchett's face. I didn't have the stomach for it.

My instinct was to get away from there and leave the body for someone else to discover. But if Mallory didn't show up, that might not be for a day or so. It was getting dark. It wasn't likely that anyone would be visiting the compound at this hour. I couldn't take a chance on leaving the dogs out there without food or water for an indefinite period.

I decided I would attend to the dogs, and then drive to the nearest public telephone to make my report. After that I would return and wait in the parking lot for the police to arrive.

I went back to the kennels. I found a hose and, not wanting to risk accidentally releasing a dog while I was fumbling with a gate, filled the water bowls by poking the hose through the metal bars. Then I grabbed a bucket of kibble from a plastic storage bin standing at one end of the yard and, reaching through the bars, tossed a handful into each dog's bowl.

In the very last run sat the Brittany spaniel who had flunked her field trials a couple of days earlier. Her gate was held closed with wire. At least I could pet her before I left. The wire untwisted easily enough. As I entered the cage, a scoop of kibble in one hand and the hose in the other, the dogs started barking again, louder than ever.

"Hush," I called. "I don't have time to visit you all." The Brittany was on her feet with hackles raised, snarling. Surely she wasn't going to bite me?

The hose was still running. Trying not to get water all over the dog, I turned slightly to see what was causing the disturbance. The next thing I knew I was shoved from behind into the dog run. Simultaneously I was aware of the sound and the feel of something hard and heavy hitting me a crack on the head. Was that a ringing in my ears or the gate clanging shut behind me? Before I could decide, the wet cement floor came up and gave me a painful whack on the nose.

. 21 .

Under Suspicion

DOG BREATH, AND the Brittany's warm tongue on my face, brought me round. I was lying in a puddle of water and my head rested in the empty kibble bowl. A bright flashlight hurt my eyes. I couldn't see who was holding it. Had Ratchett come to finish me off? But Ratchett was dead. No, it was a police officer. He helped me to my feet, but before I could thank him he had my hands behind my back and was snapping handcuffs in place.

Well, this was a first. Had I been spared only to suffer further indignities at the hands of the Surf City Police Department? I was trying to keep calm by reminding myself that I was fortunate, better handcuffs around my wrists than a dog collar around my neck, when I heard Detective Mallory's voice.

"Well, Mrs. Doolittle, did you find the dog?"

I was in no mood for his sarcasm. My head felt like a boiled owl, and lying around on wet cement hadn't done a thing for my arthritis.

"This is hardly an occasion for levity, Detective," I said. "You may not realize it, but Jim Ratchett is dead, and somebody has viciously attacked me. Would you please instruct this gentleman to remove these handcuffs?"

"Not so fast," said Mallory. "I have a few questions to ask before I turn you loose on an unsuspecting public again."

My protestations that I could answer his questions just as well, if not better, without handcuffs, cut no ice with Detective Mallory, and he ordered my captor to escort me back to the trailer.

Jim Ratchett's body was still there, just as I had found him, but the small trailer was now crowded with officials, all looking frightfully efficient as they went about doing whatever it is they do on such occasions.

We stood to one side, out of the way, while Mallory questioned me. "Now, Mrs. Doolittle, just what are you doing here?"

"My dog Watson is missing, and I had good reason to believe that Mr. Ratchett had taken her."

"I thought your dog's name was Herbie."

Well, give him credit for remembering that much at least.

"That was another dog. Mrs. Lomax's German shepherd, which she hired me to find."

"Any luck?" His interest appeared more than casual.

"Well, I thought I had tracked him to the Westgrove area, but before I had a chance to do a thorough search, I got a call from my friend in San Diego who said her dog had been kidnapped, and I went down there yesterday to help her look for it."

Thinking of Evie, I thanked my lucky stars that she was not here to see me in this absurd situation, in handcuffs. She'd probably land us both in jail.

"So that's another dog missing. Seems to me you're losing more dogs than you're finding, Mrs. Doolittle."

He had a point. I had failed miserably in my job of finding Herbie, and worse, I was responsible for the disappearance of Chamois and Watson.

Mallory seemed cordial enough, but I was still in handcuffs.

"Am I under arrest?" I asked. "You don't seriously believe I had anything to do with this killing?''

"Well, it seems mighty strange to me that every time there's a body with a dog collar around its neck, you're the first on the scene," he replied.

"I would think that the last person to see someone alive would be the prime suspect. You apparently work on the premise that it's the first person to see them dead."

While he pondered this, I seized the opportunity to continue. "And anyway, what possible motive could I have? I didn't even know Jim Ratchett, except by sight at the animal shelter. I never had occasion to speak to him until I took on Mrs. Lomax's assignment. I suggest you turn your attention to finding my assailant. Who do you think pushed me into the dog run? Or maybe you think I knocked myself out?" I'd run out of breath. I was beginning to sound like Evie. It wouldn't do to have an attack of hysterics.

Mallory took a key from his pocket and unlocked the handcuffs.

"No, Mrs. Doolittle, you are not under arrest, but . . ."

"I shall be extremely disappointed in you if you say, 'Don't leave town,' " I said, rubbing my wrists. Far from being grateful, I harboured a suspicion that he had never thought me a suspect in the first place. He was just having me on, trying to scare me into staying out of his investigation.

He grinned. "No. But I will need your statement tomorrow. Now," he looked at me with something approaching concern, "you took quite a blow to the head. I think you should have someone take a look at it. Would you like a ride to the emergency room?"

"No, thank you. I'm fine," I said, though truly I did feel a little wobbly. "Just sore and tired. It's been a long day." He really was rather nice. In other circumstances I might have found Detective Jack Mallory attractive. Looking closer, I noticed his eyes showed signs of weariness, and it occurred to me that he probably hadn't been exactly idle while I'd been chasing around after lost dogs. He was wearing jeans and a light pullover, not his customary on-the-job attire. My message must have reached him at home. No wonder he was irritated by me continuing to pop up with tales of lost dogs. But his next words chased any further such thoughts right out of my head.

"As I've told you before, Mrs. Doolittle," he was saying, "leave the detecting to us and confine yourself to dogs. In fact, you might consider taking up another line of work. You don't seem to have the knack for tracing lost pets."

If he was trying to goad me into losing my temper, he was going to be disappointed. Distraught as I was over the loss of Watson, I knew I had to appear calm and collected if I was to hope for any cooperation from the police. I tried explaining once again that it was my efforts to find Herbie, then Chamois and Watson, that had led me to the bodies of Steven Potter and Jim Ratchett.

"I wish you would at least consider the possibility that there could be some connection between the missing dogs and the murders," I said.

"You could be right," he replied. "But I doubt it. People kill out of greed, out of passion. They kill for revenge, for money, or drugs." Was he thinking about Tony? I wondered. "But I've never yet come across a killing over a dog," he concluded.

Surely the notes would convince him. Come to think of it, it was odd that he had made no mention of the break-in at my house, nor of the first warning note I had received. I wondered if Offley had even brought it to his attention.

"In that case, how do you explain the threatening notes?" I said.

"Notes? What notes?" This time he was unable to hide his interest. I told him about the three notes, and how the latest, received today, had brought me to Ratchett's place.

"Sounds like a prank," he said. "It's not likely that a murderer would take that kind of risk."

I was about to retort that where I came from committing murder was, in and of itself, considered somewhat of a risk, when he went on, "But it's advisable to take such threats seriously. You could be in danger. Take my advice, Mrs. Doolittle, and back off from this assignment. Your activities have already resulted in your getting hurt. You might not be so lucky next time."

His concern appeared genuine enough, but I was not to be so easily mollified.

"I don't believe you are really that closed-minded," I said tartly, harping back to his refusal to give my theory some consideration. "But you are certainly under no obligation to share your findings with me."

"How right you are," he replied dryly.

Very well then, this was the last time I would contact him when I was onto something. "Just one more thing, Detective," I said as he turned away.

"What is it, Mrs. Doolittle? I have a murder investigation to conduct." And a proper pig's breakfast you're making of it, too, I thought.

Aloud I said, "With Mr. Ratchett expired, there doesn't seem to be anyone in charge here. There are a dozen dogs in the kennel back there. Would you please call animal control?"

"They've already been contacted," he said. "They'll be out to pick up the dogs first thing in the morning."

I felt a little better. The dogs would be taken care of at the shelter, and some of the more presentable ones might even stand a chance of adoption.

"You're free to go, Mrs. Doolittle," said Mallory, and turned his attention back to the crime scene.

Free to go, but where? I had to find Watson and Chamois, and I had absolutely no idea where to look. Jim Ratchett had been my only lead.

Sore, tired, and gloomy, I made my way home. The blinking red light on the answering machine indicated four messages. I played them back hopefully. Maybe someone had found Watson; she was wearing an ID tag.

Beep: "This is Mrs. Jones. Do you have any news of

Tasha? Please call. I'm beginning to think we've lost her for good this time.'' Her voice sounded tearful. I knew how she felt, and was overcome with guilt that the poodle hadn't been a priority with me for the last few days.

Beep: "Dee? Evie here. It's unforgivable of you to take off like that. Call me the minute you get in." Evie, I'm doing the best I can, my dear.

Beep: "Delilah. This is Pam Harvey returning your call. I'll be at the Recreation Department tomorrow morning until ten-thirty, if you can manage to stop by." Pam was the trainer I hoped would be able to tell me more about electronic dog collars.

The last call was from Tony, saying he had checked on Watson at six a.m. that morning, and she had been fine. *"Don't worry, luv, we'll find her,"* he said. *"Meet me for breakfast in the morning and I'll give you a hand."*

Sadly I regarded Watson's old blue teddy bear lying on the kitchen floor where she had left it. It still bore traces of ketchup, and there was a tear where the vegetable knife had impaled the note. If I didn't stitch it up soon the stuffing would fall out. "Come on, Teds," I said. "Let's get you in shape for Watson when she comes home."

As I picked up the bear, I gasped. Watson had left a clue.

❖ 22 ❖
Locals Only

I SLEPT FITFULLY and was up early the next morning, glad to be released from the nightmares that had haunted my sleep like flickering pictures from a festival of old horror films. First animal control officer Mike Denver was citing me for biting Detective Mallory; then I was locked in a dog run in handcuffs. Finally, when Chamois appeared doing guard dog duty in a used-car lot, I'd had enough. It was time to get up.

Still sore from my unpleasant experience of the previous day, I eased my bruised limbs into my favourite kitchen chair and read the *Times* while I sipped my morning tea. No matter how busy I am or how eager to start my day, I can't get going without my twin fixes of tea and morning news. I sit and stare into space for ten minutes or so over the first cup. With the second I read the paper, and by the third, the brain and body begin to coordinate and I'm ready for the day to begin.

Jim Ratchett's murder, following so soon after his nephew's, had enhanced readership value in the eyes of the editor, and the report of this latest strangulation by dog collar had been given front-page status. The news item finished with a coroner's estimate that Potter had been dead approximately four or five days when his body was discovered. That would put the time of death to last Wednesday.

A quick shower. Then the bothersome daily decision of what to wear. It was always a chore, worse at this time of the year when it was so bloody hot. I was getting tired of the usual khakis, and settled on a pair of white cotton jeans and a blue shirt. I eased the hairbrush tenderly around the lump on the back of my head—a painful memento of my evening at Jim Ratchett's—then set about trying to disguisethe shadows under my eyes. Even at this early hour my makeup, such as it was, had a tendency to slide off my face due to the heat. Maybe the time was approaching when I should give up trying to dissemble, and accept my age. "Mutton dressed as lamb," my mother would sniff. On the other hand, surely deception was called for now more than ever.

I swallowed the last of the tea, rinsed the cup, and was preparing to leave when I realized my keys were not on the kitchen counter where they were supposed to be.

I returned to the bathroom where my clothes from the previous day, damp and odoriferous from my misadventures in the dog run, were still lying on the floor. No time for laundry today. Maybe I had left the keys in a pocket. No keys, but what I did find, what I had entirely forgotten about, was the item I had picked up off the floor in Jim Ratchett's trailer. It wasn't a shirt button, after all, but a small piece of enameled metal with a tiny hole at one end. It looked like it might have come from a necklace or bracelet.

The phrase "withholding evidence" came to mind. At last Mallory would have something real to accuse me of. I slipped it into my jeans pocket. Blast Mallory. I was not going to contact him again with my suspicions until I had indisputable evidence. I'd already been made to look ridiculous once. I would hand it in when I went to the police station later to sign my statement. Whenever that might be. Finding Watson was my priority now.

My keys were exactly where I had left them—in the front door. I must have been exhausted last night to have been so careless. I locked the door securely and started on my way. It was still only seven-thirty, but I knew someone who would be up and about already.

The radio surf report had said five feet and glassy. Perfect conditions, and the surfers were out in force. As I made my way to the health food bar at the corner of Main Street and PCH, I could see them paddling their boards alongside the pier, waiting for the next set.

Jan's has the best smoothies on the coast. Blended ice and fruit juice, chopped dates that clog the straw, and for me it's a meal, filling and easy to digest.

Tony came up from the beach, flecks of sand still clinging to his tanned arms and legs and damp summer wet suit, and smelling slightly of salt and surf wax. Sheepskin Ugg boots covered his spindly calves. Incongruous as they looked, teamed with surf gear, the Australian boots were very popular with surfers, offering instant comfort and warmth to feet chilled by hours in the ocean.

"Did you find her?" were his first words on spotting me. He was probably feeling responsible for Watson being missing. He repeated what he had said on my answering machine. That she was still there when he checked at six the previous morning, before he went surfing. He had fed her and told her I would be back soon. He swore he had checked that the gate was locked. I had returned from San Diego soon after noon. So she must have been snatched sometime that morning.

Tony agreed that Watson would never have gone willingly. "I tried to take her for a walk that evening after you left," he said, "but she wasn't having any. She's a one-woman dog, all right."

He had heard about Jim Ratchett's murder on the news, but there had been no mention of my involvement, and I filled him in on my harrowing adventures in the dog kennel.

The lines on his weather-beaten face etched more deeply as he expressed his concern for my safety. "You should never have gone over there by yourself, you know," he said. "Call your Uncle Tony before you go haring off next time."

He thought for a moment, then said, "So, now that bugger Ratchett's snuffed it, there goes your theory."

I sighed. "Ratchett was the only suspect I had. What's going on, Tony? There has to be somebody else involved in this. Please be honest with me. Is there anything you're not telling me? Is there anyone else who might know something? I don't care about catching the murderer. I just want to get Watson and Chamois back."

Tony swore he knew of nobody else who might have been involved. "Steve was a loner," he said. "Not a very likeable bloke. Took after his uncle there. He seemed to attract trouble. That's why most people steered clear of him."

"Well, I know for a fact he had someone with him last Tuesday evening," I said, relating the pizza delivery incident to him. "Any idea who that might have been?"

Tony shrugged. "'Aven't the foggiest," he said. "Could've been anybody. But I'll ask around to see if I can find out who Steve's been 'anging out with lately."

I still hadn't talked to Pete Kelley, the pizza delivery boy, about who or what he might have observed that night. In all the upset over Chamois' and Watson's disappearance, it kept slipping down my list of priorities. The address that Don, the assistant manager at Lotsa Lucky Pizza, had given me was just down the street from Jan's. I would stop by there before going on to the park to meet Pam Harvey.

I fingered the tender lump on my head. "The person who hit me and shoved me into the dog run probably killed Jim Ratchett, and Steven Potter, too," I said to Tony. "It's the same MO. But what's the motive? The only connection between the two is that they were related."

"And that they both worked for Jessica Lomax," Tony pointed out.

Our conversation was interrupted by a couple of young surfers who came over to ask Tony about surf conditions.

"Great. Water's the warmest it's been all year. Too many tuggos for my liking, though," he said, referring to the inland novices who flocked to the beach during the summer. "Think I'll give the Jetty a try tomorrow, or maybe even go down to Trestles."

The respect and admiration these young men showed the older man could only be won by prowess on the waves. It was the sole measure that mattered to the surfers, who could get very territorial about their local waters.

While they talked I reached into my purse for some cash to pay the bill. As I did so my hand touched something soft and unfamiliar—Watson's clue! In my haste to leave the house that morning I had quite forgotten about the scrap of torn fabric, the rip suggesting that it had been snagged by a sharp canine tooth, I had found under Watson's teddy bear the night before. I tried to remember where I had seen something like it recently, meanwhile fighting the familiar urge to jump to conclusions.

With a friendly nod to me and a "Later, dude," to Tony, the young men left, and with them my impulse to tell Tony about Watson's clue. He'd only advise me to pass the information along to Mallory. My newest theory seemed too far-fetched, even to me, to be spoken aloud without further proof. Until I could figure out a motive, I'd be better off keeping my suspicions to myself.

I told him that I was going to see Debbie again to find out more about the dog Steven had left with her, and then go by the shelter to look for Watson. "There's a chance she could have escaped her abductors and been picked up by animal control."

"But the shelter would have called you, wouldn't they?" he asked.

"Not if someone had taken her collar off." I was grasping at straws now.

Tony promised to stop by my house during the day to see if Watson had come home, and if so to keep her under lock and key until I returned.

"I think I'll pay Jessica another visit, too," I said. "Suss her out a little more. I'm beginning to think she's not told me everything. And because to start with this was simply a case of a lost or stolen dog, maybe there's something I've overlooked."

"Sounds a bit dodgy to me," he said. "You should leave it to the police."

"Don't you start," I replied, rather more tartly than I ought. "That's all I've been hearing the last few days."

"Well, you won't 'alf cop it if Mallory finds out you've gone back there," he said. "Sounds like he warned you off pretty good. Maybe once you find Watson you should chuck it in. Give up on the case, luv. It ain't worth the aggro."

Tony was right. It wasn't worth the aggravation. Except now there was much more at stake than my fee. I wasn't going to find Watson and Chamois without finding Herbie first. It was as simple as that. There was no way I could give up now.

· 23 ·

Pizza Pete

"DEEP-DISH, DOUBLE cheese, pepperoni, and sausage."
Pete evidently had total recall when it came to his pizza
deliveries.

I had located his apartment in a group of run-down pink
stucco duplexes, about half a block in from Pacific Coast
Highway, near the pier. No one had responded to my
knock, but on my way back to the car I noticed a young
man in a open garage at the rear of the building. He was
absorbed in dabbing a surfboard with wax—used by surfers
to help maintain a grip on their fiberglass boards.

Taking a chance, I called out, "Excuse me, I'm looking
for Pete Kelley?"

The young man looked up.

"That's me," he said, coming out of the garage, the
block of wax still in his hand. Tanned and barefoot, he wore
faded red shorts, white tank top, a baseball cap backward
over sun-bleached blond hair that curled around his ears.

"I'm Delilah Doolittle," I said, "I live a few blocks
down from here." I gestured vaguely south. "Don, the assistant manager at the pizza parlour, gave me your address."

"Dorky Don?" he said, grinning. "What's he want? Did

he send you to get me to go in to work? I told him when I took the job, 'When the surf's up, I'm gone, man.' ''

No wonder he couldn't afford a telephone. ''No,'' I said. ''I'm looking for a lost dog, and I hope you'll be able to help me.''

''No dogs round here.'' He pantomimed looking around.

''Not here. It was lost in Orange Blossom Heights,'' I said. ''Don told me you made a delivery last Tuesday night to the house the dog disappeared from. Maybe you can give me some more information.''

Pete remembered the dogs barking; he was scared of police dogs, he said, using the term people not familiar with the breed sometimes applied to German shepherds.

''How many dogs were there?'' I asked. If he said three, that meant that Herbie had still been there.

''I dunno. They were locked up out the back, the guy said.''

''Then how did you know they were police dogs?''

''I guessed. I saw pictures of 'em in the hall while I waited to get paid.''

''Can you remember the name of the person who ordered the pizza?''

The sweet heavy scent of coconut surrounded us as he tossed the surf wax from hand to hand while he considered the question. ''Um. It might have been Steve, real skinny little guy, he was. Yes, Steve. I remember now. He told the other guy to pay me. His friend got out his wallet, then said, 'Steve, do you have a couple of ones?' He got real mad when Steve said he didn't have any money. They both looked pretty wasted. I was glad to get out of there.''

''Did this other person have a name?'' I asked.

''Not that I remember.''

''What did he look like?''

''Tall, heavyset, shaved head. He was wearing those army fatigues.''

I would have to ask Tony if he knew anyone that fit that description.

"And they paid cash?" I said.

"Yeah. We don't take checks or credit cards."

If I had been hoping for a paper trail, I was out of luck.

"One other thing," I asked. "Do you remember seeing a car or van in the driveway?"

"Nope. Parked there myself."

Not much to go on, I thought as I headed toward the park. Nice young man, though. I was glad he wasn't the one who'd wound up dead in the doghouse. But I was no closer to finding out who Steven's companion was that night. Whoever he was, could he have been mad enough at Steven to kill him? Pete had said they were "wasted." I supposed that meant they'd been drinking, or taking drugs. In that case, anything was possible.

• 24 •

Puppy Kindergarten

TALKING TO PETE had taken longer than anticipated, and Puppy Kindergarten was already in progress when I drove into the Recreation Center parking lot.

Pam waved when she saw me and signalled "five minutes" with her hand. She had been around dogs all her life and, though still in her twenties, knew dog training as well as anyone I knew. Her parents, now retired, had bred Samoyeds for many years, and Pam had cut her teeth on a Nylabone. Dressed in crisp white shorts and a bright blue tee shirt bearing the Surf City logo, her firm, tanned legs rising saucily out of black socks and boots, she epitomized the ideal California golden girl. Her hair, which hung in a heavy plait, was bleached and dry from sun and chlorine. On summer vacation from UC Davis where she was studying to be a vet, she was earning her tuition by working for Surf City Parks & Recreation, dividing her time between dog training here in the park and life-guarding at the city pool.

I sat down at a redwood picnic table to watch the class while I waited. A dozen or so pups and their handlers were lined up in two rows facing each other. The dogs ranged in size and age from a miniature Doxie, barely eight weeks old, to a boisterous German shepherd of about four months.

"Forward six paces, halt, sit, praise, stand," Pam called, putting her students through their paces. When the two rows met there was a confusion of wagging tails and dodging feet, as handlers, intent on watching their pets' responses, collided with their opposite numbers. Most of the dogs appeared to catch on quicker than their owners who, whether preteen or retiree, were like proud parents in wanting their pets to do well.

The shepherd pup, evidently the class clown, circled his owner's legs with the leash. In his confusion the owner, a tall young man in jeans and a white long-sleeved cotton shirt, dropped the leash, and the pup ran off to make the acquaintance of a fluffy Bichon Frise. This, in turn, broke the concentration of the Bichon's owner, a pretty young woman in a long skirt, sun top, and floppy straw hat, and set off a domino effect of canine disobedience.

Pam gave the class an opportunity to get the excess of high spirits out of their systems.

"Take five. Let your dogs socialize. And don't forget to scoop the poop," she called, as she joined me.

"Did you find Watson yet?" she asked as soon as we'd said our hellos. "Couldn't believe it when I saw your ad in the paper this morning." I had called in the ad when I arrived home the previous afternoon, and had got it in just under the deadline.

"Unfortunately no," I said. "But I'm working on it."

"Don't worry, you'll find her if anybody can," she said consolingly.

She gave me a bright smile. "Whatever you wanted to talk to me about must be pretty important to tear you away from your search."

"Well, it's all kind of tied together," I said, not wanting to take the time to explain. "But what I wanted to ask is what you know about electronic collars. Something to do with the case I'm working on."

"What kind?" she said.

"You mean there's more than one?"

"Oh, yes." She pushed her blond bangs back under her sun visor. "There's the bark collar, that gives the dog a slight jolt every time he barks. They're very popular these days," she sighed. "So many lonely dogs left alone all day to bark and annoy the neighbours."

As we talked, she kept an appraising eye on her students, relaxing in the shade of the picnic pavilion. At the water fountain, the owners of the shepherd and the Bichon were deep in conversation, unmindful of the playful pups wrestling at their feet. A romance in the making, perhaps?

"There's another collar that's used with the so-called invisible fencing," Pam continued. "And then there's the training collar. They all work on much the same negative stimulation principle. The dog barks, steps over a boundary, responds incorrectly, and gets a jolt."

"It's the training collar I'm interested in. Do you use them?"

"Heavens no." She looked at me in surprise.

"Are they dangerous, then?" I asked.

She thought for a moment, a slight frown appearing between her delicately arched eyebrows. "I've never heard of any incidents of physical damage," she said. "But I don't like them because they make the dog fearful. Instead of working for praise, the dog is motivated out of fear of getting zapped. There's no interaction. Praise is so important. A dog only wants to please," she said, warming to her subject. "I mean, that's the wonderful thing about working with animals, the bonding, the mutual affection."

She looked over to where a couple of the handlers were practicing the sit/praise/stand routine. "Be firm!" she called to the Doxie's owner as, in response to the sit command, the little dog rolled over on its back. "Let her know who's boss."

Yes, well, we could all see who was going to be the boss in that household.

Pam turned back to me. "There's always the risk that

electronic collars can be misused, or overused, though other trainers have told me that they can be quite effective when used correctly. It's like everything else. It depends on the skill of the trainer. You have to know what you're doing.''

"Do you think a training collar could harm a human?'' I asked.

"Real harm? No. Might cause some discomfort, though why anyone would . . .'' She broke off, struck by a sudden thought.

"It's funny,'' she said, "you're the second person to ask me that question this week.''

• 25 •

Debbie Comes Clean

DESPITE THE SEPTEMBER heat, I shivered. My experience at Ratchett's kennel last night was all too recent and vivid, my nerves were on edge, and Pam's comment was a chilly reminder that I was walking in a killer's shadow. Someone else inquiring about electronic collars might be a perfectly innocent coincidence. Except I didn't believe in coincidences.

"Oh," I said, trying to sound casual. "Who else?"

"A police detective. Mallory, I think his name was."

I breathed again. Of course, Mallory. I really hadn't thought much about what direction his inquiries might be taking him. On this occasion, at least, he was way ahead of me.

"Hey, are you two working on the same case?" asked Pam, her cornflower-blue eyes shining with excitement.

"Well, sort of. The dog I'm looking for is involved in a case that Detective Mallory's working on."

"Well, you be careful. Got to go now, before they forget what they've learned. Hope you find Watson soon." With a wave she turned back to her class.

Most of the puppies had settled down somewhat after their time out, and now sat obediently beside their handlers awaiting the command, "Forward six paces..." That command was delayed, however, while the German shepherd's owner ran after his dog, now in hot pursuit of a seagull that had rashly landed nearby. The chase was in full cry when I left. I didn't wait to see the outcome. I had quarry of my own to pursue.

DEBBIE WAS NEXT. I had to know what Steven had told her about Herbie—if indeed it was Herbie that he had left with her the night before he was killed. Maybe she hadn't told me the whole truth. I only half suspected her of knowingly being involved in Herbie's dognapping. She was a dreamer, not a schemer. If anything she was a victim herself, reacting to whatever life laid at her door, slow to take matters into her own hands. But I was convinced she knew more about this whole business than she had so far let on.

It felt strange driving around without Watson. I missed her intelligent responses to my theorizing—the cock of her head, the sharp ears alert to my every vocal nuance. I tried not to think about what might have happened to her and Chamois. About if, perish the thought, they might have been done away with already. The person who had stolen the dogs was, in all likelihood, the same person who had committed two murders. What would stop them from killing a couple of animals?

Fortunately, my arrival at the approach to Debbie's street brought an end to such dismal speculation.

I drove slowly, taking care to avoid a bunch of skateboarders making the most of the waning days of summer vacation. It was too bad there wasn't somewhere other than the street to practice their manoeuvres. I parked the wagon under the same water-starved oleander outside Debbie's apartment. Even drought-tolerant trees were beginning to show the effects of the September heat.

As I got out of the car, Debbie came gliding toward me on in-line skates, a sallow-faced youth in tow, who she introduced as Kevin. The two days that had passed since I last saw her had done nothing to improve her appearance, though the moussed spikes had taken on an orange hue, and a pink butterfly now adorned her left cheek.

She appeared uncomfortable to see me, and no doubt my determined air, quite different from the solicitous attitude I had shown the first time we met, gave her cause to be on her guard.

"Hi." Getting straight to the point, I asked, "Out looking for that dog?"

"Nah. He's long gone," she replied. Her unconcern seemed genuine.

"German shepherd, didn't you say it was?" I persisted. She hesitated, looking as if she might glide off again.

I decided to gamble on my hunch that the dog was indeed Herbie. "Look," I fibbed, "the police think there may be a connection between the missing dog and the murders of Steven and your uncle."

At the mention of the police Kevin had edged away and was now leaning on the far side of my car, smoking a cigarette.

"You heard about Uncle Jim then?" Debbie asked.

"Yes, I did. I'm so sorry, my dear." No need to tell her that I had discovered both her brother's and her uncle's bodies. Though I had no tears to shed over the premature demise of the disagreeable Mr. Ratchett, I did feel sorry for the girl, losing two close members of her family in such a brief period.

"It must be very hard for you, so soon after Steven," I went on. "But don't you see, there's got to be a connection, and the only one I can see is the dog. You might be in danger yourself. And how long do you think it will be before the police figure out that you've been harbouring stolen property, because that's what the dog is?"

Debbie's eyes widened in alarm. "But I didn't do anything wrong," she protested.

"Of course you didn't." I softened immediately as I saw the tears well up. I'm no good at strong-arm tactics. "But don't you see, if people aren't aware of the truth, they'll more than likely suspect the worst." A couple of noisy skateboarders swooped toward us on the sidewalk, daring us not to move out of their path. "Look, can't we go inside and talk about this?" I said.

She thought for a moment, then, leaning against the oleander, unfastened her skates.

"See you later, Kev," she said, dismissing her friend.

I followed as she padded barefoot into the apartment, and waited while she put her skates away. She went to the refrigerator and pulled out a can of beer, not offering me anything. That was okay. This wasn't a social call, and I'd have to be a lot thirstier than I was before I could drink beer out of a can, or out of a crystal goblet, come to that.

She leaned against the refrigerator door. I waited a moment or two for an invitation to sit down, then, none being forthcoming, brushed away the crumbs from a plastic chair cracked and mottled with age, and sat down at the tiny kitchen table.

"Steven didn't have a car," I said. "How did he get the dog here?"

"Someone gave him a ride," she said. Then, before I could ask, she added, "I don't know who it was. He stayed in the car. Was in a real hurry, too. Kept honking the horn."

"You knew it was a man, though?"

She giggled. "Steve didn't have no girlfriends. Couldn't afford it."

She moved over to a small mirror hanging above the kitchen sink, leaned forward and, turning her head to one side, touched the pink butterfly admiringly.

"What day was that?" I asked.

Still looking in the mirror, she pulled thoughtfully at her spikey hair. "Last Tuesday. I remember, 'cause I'd been to the pier with Kevin. We always go there for the band Tuesday evenings."

The same night as the pizza delivery. Whoever drove

Steven to Debbie's was in all likelihood the same person who later that evening shared his pizza. I wondered if the police were onto him yet.

"About what time was that?" I asked Debbie.

"We came back early. Band wasn't very good, and I was getting cold." It did get cool by the water once the sun went down, even in our warmest weather, I knew. "So we were back soon after it got dark," she continued. "Steve arrived about ten minutes after Kevin left."

"What did he tell you about the dog?" I asked.

She turned from the mirror, tears welling up. She was obviously reluctant to say anything negative about her dead brother. But I was not about to be put off.

"Tell me what you know, help me find the dog, and it will go easier for you." I took another gamble. "Perhaps the police need never find out that Steven planned to hold the dog for ransom."

That hit home. She made no effort to deny it. Steven had told her to take care of the dog for a few days until Mrs. Lomax got back. "He said it could mean money, real money," she said. "We could move out of this place, get a car, everything."

My suspicions were confirmed. "So you knew the dog belonged to Mrs. Lomax?" I could barely conceal my excitement.

"Yes. I tried to make him take it back, but he goes, 'It's too late, it's done now.'" She sipped her beer. "He said the old lady was worth a lot of money, and why should Uncle Jim get all the gravy."

Why indeed, I thought.

She had put the dog out on the patio with some food Steven had brought with him. Herbie, not surprisingly, had escaped at the first opportunity.

"I never had a chance to tell Steven," she said. "And once I knew he was dead, it, like, just didn't seem important anymore. I was glad the dog was gone. That way nobody could say I stole him."

That explained Herbie. But I still couldn't see a motive for the murders. I wondered if Debbie knew anything else, or had observed anything that might put her in danger. Two close family members were dead. The "family fortune" motive came back to mind.

"Can you think of any reason anyone would want your uncle and Steven dead?"

"Like what?" she asked sullenly, tipping up the can to get the last of the beer.

"Well. Is there any money or property that they or another family member might inherit?"

She sighed. "There's nothing. And there's only me left." She raised her eyebrows speculatively. "Though I suppose I'll get the guard dog business. I hadn't thought of that. But I don't think it's worth much without Uncle Jim. No. I'm the only one left now," she repeated wanly. She was indeed a pathetic figure in her bare feet, her skimpy shorts, and a white bikini top wrapping her pale, spare body like a bandage.

"The only rich person I know is Mrs. Lomax," she continued, adding as an afterthought, "I think she was a partner or something in Uncle Jim's business."

That didn't sound very likely. "What makes you say that?"

"Steven told me that once when Uncle Jim was drunk he told him that Jessica was, like, a silent partner. Said it in a funny way. But Steven said he didn't believe it."

"What do you think he meant, 'funny'?" Jim Ratchett was the most humourless man I had ever met.

"I don't know." She shrugged.

I didn't think she could tell me much more, but I made sure she still had my telephone number, in case anything else occurred to her, and went on my way. As I rounded the corner at one end of the street, I thought I caught a glimpse in the rearview mirror of Detective Mallory's car entering the street from the other direction. Mindful of Tony's warning, I kept my fingers crossed that Debbie would not mention my having just been to see her. This little visit would hardly be considered "staying out of police business."

BY THE TIME I reached the shelter it was nearing the five o'clock closing hour. I had just started checking the runs for Herbie, Watson, and Chamois when Rita came out of the office and beckoned to me.

"I tried to call you," she said. "There's a good-looking shepherd came in this afternoon. Kennel seventy-nine. Picked up in the Westgrove area. Could be the one you're looking for."

· 26 ·

Herbie, Is That You?

"A YOUNG MAN brought him in," Rita went on, as we walked toward the area where the large dogs were housed. "Said he found him at the corner of Acacia and Magnolia in Westgrove." With her long blond hair and brightly coloured outfits—vivid shades of pink and orange today—Rita provided a pleasant contrast against the gloomy background of the concrete and metal shelter.

"One thing doesn't seem right, though," she continued, consulting her clipboard. "We always scan for microchips, and we got a positive on this dog. But when we tried to reach the owner, the phone number came back negative, no longer in service. The vet who did the implant told us the owner moved away several years ago and left no forwarding address."

"What name is the dog registered to?" I asked.

"A Reeves Robertson, of San Juan Capistrano," she replied.

"It can't be the dog I'm looking for then," I said with certainty. "My client never mentioned it having a chip. And, anyway, she bred him herself," I added lamely. How could I be sure of anything anymore?

Surely Jessica would have mentioned if Herbie had a

microchip? A lot of breeders and pet owners use them these days. It's a more reliable method of proving ownership than a tattoo that can fade in time. The chip is injected with a syringe and bears a number registered to both the owner and the veterinarian who does the implant.

"I thought microchips were supposed to be foolproof," I said.

"Only if the owner notifies the vet when they move, so he can change his records," Rita explained. "In this case it looks like the original owner either moved or gave the dog away, and no one bothered to change the records. Or maybe they died. We'll probably never know."

The speculations were endless.

Rita, in high heels and a tight short skirt, could not keep pace with me as I hurried through the shelter. By the time she caught up with me I had already taken Herbie's photo from my purse and was comparing it with the German shepherd in kennel seventy-nine.

It could be Herbie. He bore a strong resemblance to Major and Sheba, Jessica's other dogs. The alert, fearless expression, the noble head, the strong, well-muscled body all announced champion and made the dog a standout among the mostly mixed breeds in the neighbouring pens. But Herbert Fitzherbert, best of breed? What about the microchip? I played back in my mind the several times I had asked Jessica about identification. She'd had every opportunity to mention it. She never had.

Something wasn't right. This dog certainly looked like Herbie, and he was picked up in the right location, but if it was Jessica's dog, then why did he have a microchip implant registered to somebody else? Jessica's reputation as a breeder was based on her having bred her own line for several generations.

Was it a coincidence, a look-alike that just happened to have been found in Westgrove? No. I don't believe in coincidences; experience has taught me that things happen for a reason. Perhaps someone wanted me to think it was Herbie. A similar dog intentionally planted at the shelter to throw me off the trail? But that didn't seem very likely. Jessica would know immediately that it wasn't her dog.

Another thought occurred. Was it possible that the young man who claimed to have found the dog was Debbie's friend Kevin? Again the suspicion came to mind that Debbie might have passed the dog along to an accomplice. I remembered how uncomfortable Kevin had become earlier at the mention of the police. Maybe he'd been holding the dog for her, but they'd got cold feet and he had turned it in, saying he "found" it. I dismissed that idea. He'd be more likely to drop off the dog in a strange neighbourhood, rather than risk being identified by bringing it to the shelter.

A scrap of a thought fluttered through my mind, at first so nebulous that I had trouble putting it into words.

I turned to Rita. "If the dog had been impounded here before, with the chip in it, and was adopted by a new owner, would you have a record of that?"

She nodded, her pink and orange plastic cat earrings swinging in agreement. "I see where you're going," she said. "Well, if he came in with a chip on a previous occasion, we would have gone through the same procedure, trying to contact the owner, and coming up empty. If he was then adopted out, it would be up to the new owner to reregister the dog."

That obviously had not been done in this case. I wondered how much work would be involved in checking back through past impound records to trace the new owner, if indeed the dog had been in before.

"Tell you what," said Rita, reading my thoughts. "Why don't I see if someone has time to look through the records for you? Check with me before you leave." She headed back to the office.

Mulling it all over, I toured the rest of the shelter in a halfhearted search for Chamois and Watson. The newer impounds looked at me expectantly as I passed, hoping for a deliverance which the old-timers, with their resigned expressions, seemed to know would probably never come. Occasionally, when a kennel attendant would take out a dog and lead him away, the other dogs would bark as he trotted down the walkway, putting me in mind of those old movies where the guys in the big house would cheer a fellow inmate with chants of encouragement as he was led away to the chair.

Not for the first time I cursed all irresponsible pet owners. Why didn't they care? But I was a fine one to talk. Wasn't it through my own carelessness that I was here now, looking for my own dog? And Evie's?

I searched on. Peering into the back of the runs where the small dogs often hide; double-checking the large dog cages for Watson. She was a smart dog. There was always the possibility that she might have escaped her captors. She would be watching their every move, and at the first opportunity would be out the door. Or, if she had proved too troublesome, she might simply have been abandoned on the street and subsequently picked up by animal control.

Anything was possible.

It certainly was. In that strange serendipitous way in which, when you're looking for one thing you find something else you'd almost given up on, it wasn't Watson and Chamois I found, but Tasha Jones, the delinquent poodle. Even though two weeks of wandering had taken its toll of the usually well-groomed white dog, there was no question that the shaggy grey mop sitting in the last run of the small dog section was the wayward Tasha. I'd know her anywhere, and she recognized me with a happy yelp, seemingly not in the least dismayed to discover herself in such surroundings, as if she knew I would find her eventually.

On my return to the office to put a hold on Tasha, ensuring she would be kept for Mrs. Jones to pick up the following day, Rita looked up with a smile.

"We've traced the adopting owner of the shepherd," she said. "Does the name Jessica Lomax mean anything to you?"

✦ 27 ✦

Massive In Mauve

HERBERT FITZHERBERT A pound hound? With bogus papers? No wonder Jessica had been so adamant that I find the dog before he reached the shelter. Molly's words came back to me. "Easy enough to make up false papers," she had said. "Just use the pedigree of a similar dead animal." Jessica wouldn't want it to get out that Herbie wasn't the aristocrat she was passing him off to be. She knew the shelter scanned for microchips. And if she was working here at the time the dog was originally impounded, she would have known that he had a chip implant.

But why would a breeder of her reputation do such a thing? Some kind of insurance scam? Was that the "business" she and Ratchett were in that Debbie had alluded to? Jessica just didn't seem the type, and I wasn't sure there was enough money involved in insuring show dogs to make the risk worthwhile.

It was all very confusing, and there was only one way to sort it out. Jessica would have to come to the shelter to identify the dog herself.

It was too late for her to get to the shelter today, however. The five-minute warning that the place was about to close had already been announced over the public address system. Kennel attendants were doing the rounds, tossing stainless steel feeding bowls into the concrete runs with nerve-shattering accuracy, causing the more timid dogs to back away in fear. Cleaning, along with the grim task of euthanizing the unadoptable animals, would take place first thing in the morning—uncomfortably reminiscent of executions at sunrise—before the shelter opened.

I tried to call Jessica, but her line was busy, so I decided to drive over to Orange Blossom Heights and give her the good news in person. It would give me an excuse to let her know that I was aware she hadn't been entirely honest with me. Though the fact that she had doctored Herbie's pedigree was really none of my business. He was her legal property. She had hired me to find her dog. I had found him. All that was left was for me to collect my fee.

I HAD TO park a little way down the street, out of sight of the house. Because of the hour, more people were about, and in this semirural area of winding lanes, parking was allowed on one side of the street only.

Everything looked just the same as it did the first time I arrived at the peaceful cul-de-sac. The yellow police tape was gone, and there was no evidence of the gruesome event that had taken place there just a few days before. The Winnebago was still in the driveway, though the door was closed this time. The only change I could see was that there was now a ''for sale'' sign planted on the front lawn.

Opening the front door in response to my knock, Jessica, massive in mauve, was surprised and seemed a little put out to see me. I wondered why she always wore those long skirts. Maybe she didn't have good legs, or couldn't be bothered to shave them. Certainly the skirts added a dramatic and flamboyant touch to an otherwise rigid persona. The huge German shepherd pendant still adorned her ample bosom, but the matching earrings had been replaced by plain silver hoops. Sheba and Major stood patiently at her side.

"Mrs. Doolittle," she said in her usual imperious manner. "This is most inconvenient. I'm in the middle of preparing dinner, and I'm expecting an important call from my realtor. You'd better come into the kitchen. I hope you've brought news of my Herbie."

She led the way into the comfortable, bright kitchen, familiar from that long evening we had shared there the day we found poor Steven Potter in the doghouse. A delicious savoury aroma emanating from a large pot simmering on the back of the electric stove reminded me that I'd had nothing to eat since the smoothie at Jan's early that morning. The two tabbies were still dozing, one in a laundry basket in the corner, the other in a pool of evening sunlight on the broad window ledge above the kitchen sink.

I didn't tell Jessica my news straightaway. There were still some unanswered questions. "Tell me," I hedged. "Did Herbie have a microchip implant?"

She sidestepped in turn. "Herbie never runs away," she said. "I blame myself for leaving him when I went to San Diego. He must have been scared off during the murder. In fact, the more I think about it, the more I am convinced that the murderer killed that unfortunate young man in order to steal Herbie."

"You don't think that's a bit far-fetched?" I said. I was beginning to sound like Detective Mallory.

"Mrs. Doolittle, I don't know what you're doing here, asking me these ridiculous questions. I am paying you to find my dog. Your time would be much better employed by doing all you can to that end."

"Well, as a matter of fact, that's why I'm here," I responded. "There's a dog at the shelter that looks very much like Herbie. Only thing is, this dog has a microchip implant. That's why I was asking. If Herbie wasn't wearing a chip, then I'll just have to keep looking. However, if you think it might be Herbie, you'll have to go over there and identify him. I tried to call you, but your line was busy. The shelter's closed now, but I can meet you there first thing in the morning.''

Fiery red blotches broke out on her face and spread on up onto her white scalp, clashing with her tightly permed and thinning orange hair. She looked perturbed and angry at the same time.

''I thought I told you I didn't want him to go to the shelter,'' she snapped. Major and Sheba, sensing their owner's alarm, moved restlessly. Then, displaying superb self-control, Jessica recovered herself and went on, ''I would very much have liked to have kept him away from there.'' She almost whispered the words. There was no attempt to deny it was Herbie.

The telephone provided a welcome interruption for both of us. There was a phone in the kitchen, but she opted to use the extension in the hall, the dogs trotting behind her.

The tempting aroma from the steaming pot had set my mouth watering. I couldn't resist taking a peek. Marrow bones, rice, garlic, onions, and carrots. It was more than I could bear. I could hear Jessica carrying on in her usual domineering fashion about whelping boxes and the merits of various veterinarians. I picked up the ladle from the spoon rest. Surely she wouldn't begrudge me a taste?

The spoon fell from my fingers with a clatter, as Jessica suddenly reentered the room.

''That's a special recipe I make up for the dogs,'' she said. ''I prefer to cook it myself. That commercial stuff from the store is just so much junk food.''

Before I could cover my embarrassment, the telephone intruded a second time, and with a sigh and a murmured ''Excuse me,'' Jessica flounced off once more. This time, from the snatches of conversation I could overhear, she was talking to her realtor.

Startled awake by the spoon clattering onto the tile floor, one of the cats was now rearranging herself in the laundry basket, kneading a nest on one of Jessica's colourful skirts. The fabric looked familiar. In fact, it looked suspiciously like the scrap I had found with Watson's teddy bear. With a mounting sense of foreboding, coupled with a healthy dose of caution, I gently eased the cat to one side for a closer look, keeping one eye on the doorway while inspecting the voluminous skirt with the other. Finally I found what I was looking for—a small rent in the hem, barely noticeable in the colorful yardage. Jessica may not even have been aware of it herself. I hurriedly stuffed the skirt back in the basket as I heard her winding down the conversation.

Now what? Should I confront her? Demand to know what she'd done with my dog? I thought not. She could come up with half a dozen different reasons for the tear in her skirt, and certainly would deny ever having been in my kitchen. I needed more than a tear in a frock before I could accuse Jessica of stealing my dog. Or worse.

The other cat was now playing with something she had found on the window ledge. Dabbing it with her paw, she knocked it into the sink. Retrieving it I saw that it was one of the German shepherd earrings with the jointed limbs that Jessica had been wearing the day we met. One of the legs was missing.

♣ 28 ♣

Prime Suspect

WITH TREMBLING FINGERS I took from my jeans pocket the piece of jewelry I had found in Ratchett's office the day of his death, though I scarcely needed to make the comparison to know that I had a match.

Fear pricked my armpits as I fitted the two pieces together. Cold perspiration trickled down my back while questions and half-formed answers swirled around in my head. Was Jessica somehow involved in Ratchett's murder? I felt faint. I had to get out of there. But I barely had time to replace the earring on the window ledge before I heard her hang up the phone.

"Very well, Mrs. Doolittle," Jessica said as she came back into the kitchen. "I suppose I'd better take a look at this dog you claim to be Herbie." Had she seen me with the earring? I didn't think so. Her attention was taken with holding the door open for the two dogs at her heels. It could have been my discomfort that I might have been caught prying again that made me think I detected a sly look in her eye, a certain oddness in her manner, as she continued, "I'll meet you at the shelter tomorrow morning as soon as it opens. Ten o'clock."

It sounded like a dismissal, and I was only too glad to

be dismissed before I, too, found myself being fitted for an electronic dog collar.

The front door had barely slammed behind me, when it dawned on me what I had done. In my haste I had left the incriminating piece of jewelry on the window ledge along with its counterpart. Well, there was no going back now. Nothing for it but to press on regardless.

The light was fading as I made my way to my car, where I sat and tried to figure out what to do next, fighting the familiar urge to jump to conclusions. That's what had got me in trouble before. The earring alone didn't necessarily mean anything. Jessica could have dropped it at Ratchett's at any time. His trailer floor looked like it hadn't been swept for months. But I had seen her wearing those same earrings only a week ago. Unless she possessed an identical pair, she had to have lost the piece during the past few days. But she might have had a perfectly innocent and legitimate reason to visit Ratchett. Perhaps to offer condolences on Steven's death, or to settle her pet-sitting account.

But there seemed no plausible explanation for the scrap of fabric I had found in my kitchen other than that Jessica, either acting alone or with an accomplice, had taken Watson. Of course, I realized belatedly, Ratchett wasn't the only dog expert in this case. Jessica also would know how to lure a reluctant animal away from home. And she took Chamois, too, there could be no question of that. The three notes had undoubtedly been authored by the same person, all bearing the same stamp of irrationality.

If Jessica had killed Ratchett, then who had killed Steven? Jessica was in San Diego at the time. The police must have checked out that alibi.

And where were Watson and Chamois? Jessica might have killed Ratchett, and good riddance, some might say. But she wouldn't kill the dogs. I was sure of that. No, they were still alive. Possibly locked up somewhere in the outbuildings here.

Perhaps if I'd been thinking more clearly I wouldn't have

done what I did next. The thought of the two murders should have given me pause.

Taking a flashlight from the glove compartment, and tucking my purse out of sight under the seat, I locked the car and headed back to Jessica's.

The blinds were drawn. With any luck I could make my way around to the side of the house unobserved.

It was with a sense of déjà vu that I checked the out-buildings. It was a week to the day, almost to the hour, that I had made this same inspection tour while looking for Herbie. I first checked the dog run. That would seem to be the most secure place to confine a dog. It was empty. And spotless. No sign of food or droppings to indicate that a dog had been there recently.

Cautiously I eased open the side door to the garage, aware that the slightest noise might alert Sheba and Major. The door creaked, and I stopped and listened. All I could hear was the low murmur of the television in the kitchen. Not a sound from Sheba and Major. They were too busy wolfing down that stew Jessica had so lovingly prepared for them. It was a lovely, comfortable home. What could possibly be at stake that Jessica would risk so much? Why was she moving?

So many questions, and no answers.

Carefully closing the garage door behind me, I made my way across the yard to the horse barn. Now out of direct line of sight from the house, I was confident nobody could see me, and I would be safe unless the dogs came out. Jessica would probably put them outside after they had finished eating, so I had better not linger too long.

Tack, moldering and rusting with age, ghostly reminders of equine occupants long gone, swayed and rattled against the wall as I pushed open the heavy barn door. Dust motes danced in the dim beam of the flashlight, which was barely strong enough to reach into the furthest corners.

"Watson," I whispered. The only answer was the rus-tling of a small rodent, eking out a living from remnants of hay, of which a faint scent still clung to the dusty air.

The silence was broken by the sound of the back door opening. Was Jessica letting the dogs out? I held my breath until I heard the rattle of a trash can lid, and the door closing again. I peered through the grimy barn window until I was sure the dogs had not followed her out, and then, defeated, I gave up the search. Wherever Jessica had stashed Watson and Chamois, it wasn't on these premises. I cautiously made my way back alongside the house to the street.

As I skirted the Winnebago, I heard a dog whimpering. Must be one of Jessica's shepherds, I thought, though the sound didn't seem to be coming from the house. I started to move on, but there it was again.

It was coming from the motor home. I made my way around to the other side, away from the house, so that if Jessica should happen to look out she wouldn't see me standing on tiptoe to peer into the motor home window. The mini-blinds were down, but one of the slats had caught on something inside, raising it a little, just enough to give me a small peephole. The only light was from a streetlamp, but I thought I could see the shape of a dog. Was it Watson, or was my imagination playing tricks in the half-light? As I strained my eyes for a better look, I saw something white and furry. It had to be Chamois. Then Watson, getting my scent, was on her feet, shaking, rattling her collar, ready to go.

All fears forgotten now, I tried the coach door. Locked, of course. I looked around for something heavy to smash the window. But that would bring Jessica out, and I would be no match for her if it came to a scuffle.

I would have to come back with reinforcements, preferably in the shape of Detective Mallory and Officer Offley.

Back in my car, I drove to the all-night market at the corner of the road leading into Jessica's neighbourhood to telephone for help. Detective Mallory wasn't available, said the officer who answered the phone. Would I like to leave a message? What message could I, should I leave? That I'd found a stolen dog? Tell about torn skirts and broken jewelry, and that I suspected Jessica of murdering Ratchett, possibly Steven Potter as well? There was no way to convey it all in a message without sounding ludicrous, or worse, hysterical.

Finally, deciding that brevity, being not only the soul of wit but the heart of clarity, would best suit my purpose, and would leave less room for misinterpretation, I said, "Please inform Detective Mallory that Mrs. Doolittle has traced her stolen dogs to the Lomax residence, and that the Lomax dog is at the animal shelter." I trusted Mallory would draw the right conclusions.

"Dogs, eh?" said the officer. "Let me give you the number for animal control."

"This has nothing to do with animal control," I said, keeping a firm grip on my temper though I felt like screaming with frustration. "Please see that Detective Mallory gets the message. It is of the utmost importance."

I then placed a call to Evie. She was not there either, but I left a message with Rosa to the effect that I had located Chamois and would call her again as soon as I had my hands on him.

Then I drove back to Jessica's. Luckily my parking space was still vacant. Even if she came out on the driveway and looked down the street, Jessica wouldn't be able to see my car tucked around the corner of the winding lane.

It was no use waiting for Mallory to show up. Jessica could take off with Watson and Chamois at any time. I would have to rescue the dogs myself. I checked in the back of the wagon for some kind of pry tool. Out of all the equipment I carried around with me nothing seemed suitable. In desperation I dumped out the knitting bag, still in the car after my San Diego trip. While not as versatile as a Swiss army knife, a large gauge aluminum knitting needle was better than nothing.

By now it was completely dark, and I felt a little less conspicuous as I once again made my way back to the

Winnebago armed with flashlight, knitting needle, and a nail file I had taken from my purse. I tried the door again. Still locked, of course. I attempted to force it open with the knitting needle, but the door was flush with the coach exterior and there was no opening large enough.

Watson whimpered again. "Good girl," I said. She started to get agitated when she heard my voice. "Hush," I said. "Hang on, we'll soon get you out of there."

But how? I made my way around the motor home looking for a means of entry. At the rear an aluminum ladder accessed the rooftop luggage rack and the air-conditioning unit. Perhaps I could pry that open and enter the coach from above without making too much commotion. Once in, I would be able to unlock the door from the inside, and with any luck make my getaway with the dogs without being spotted.

I climbed onto the roof and set to work, loosening screws with the nail file, jabbing in the knitting needle wherever I could, with the object of loosening the air conditioner cover. With that out of the way I should be able to stamp my foot through the roof. So intent was I on my task that I didn't hear Jessica until her heavy tread crunched on the gravel path a few feet away. I stopped what I was doing. I felt rather than heard the coach door open. Watson's snarl was quickly followed by the sound of the engine turning over.

The Winnebago started to move.

• 29 •

Delilah's Wild Ride

IT DIDN'T TAKE long to determine where Jessica was going. As soon as the motor home rumbled up the westbound freeway on-ramp I guessed we were headed for the animal shelter. Less easy to figure out was how to keep from being thrown off the roof of the Winnebago as it gathered speed to merge with the fast-moving traffic. As Jessica moved into the fast lane I rolled from side to side like a rag doll. All I had to hold on to was the low luggage rack running the perimeter of the roof. I quickly discovered that the only way to keep from sliding off was to maintain a low profile, lying spread-eagled on my stomach, clinging to the railing at the back, with my feet wedged against the railing at the side.

When Jessica had interrupted me, I had made considerable progress on loosening the air conditioner cover. All it needed was a good kick to finish the job. Now, as the traffic slowed for a stalled vehicle by the centre divider, I tried kicking from a prone position. But when the Winnebago suddenly lurched ahead, I found myself struggling to regain a safe grip. I gave up the attempt altogether when it occurred to me that even if I succeeded in getting the cover off and stamping a hole in the roof, I would end up inside the Winnebago with Jessica. Not such a good idea after all.

When I was not preoccupied with hanging on for dear life, I speculated on what Jessica planned to do when she got to the shelter—assuming, of course, that she had a plan and was not acting out of blind panic.

Save Herbie from euthanasia? But there was no chance he would be included with the morning's batch. His microchip ID guaranteed him a full week before any disposition would be made. She would know that.

Why would she risk stealing her own dog when for the sake of a few hours she could claim him legally in the morning?

Clearly she was leaving nothing to chance.

The traffic slowed again at the interchange with the northbound freeway, and I tried to attract attention by waving to a group of surfers riding in the back of a pickup truck. Their cheery "Way to go, lady!" as the pickup dodged through the traffic and darted ahead was encouraging but not exactly what I'd had in mind. What else did I expect? In a place where bungee-jumping grandmothers and octogenarian sky divers are commonplace, the sight of a woman, albeit of a certain age, riding atop a posh motor home was hardly remarkable.

Any further thoughts I might have had of alerting the attention of a passing motorist were abandoned at this point, as once again the traffic speeded up, Jessica changed lanes, and it took every ounce of my strength and concentration to maintain my grip to keep from being hurled into the traffic.

After a few miles of what remains to this day the most terrifying transit experience of my life, I risked raising my head to check on our progress. And almost immediately put it down again. Even on a balmy September night, at sixty miles an hour the wind was most unpleasant, blowing dust in my face, grit in my eyes, and exhaust fumes in my nostrils and mouth. But in those few seconds I had seen, from my vantage point above the freeway, the flood control channel which ran along the rear of both Jessica's and Ratchett's places, had glimpsed a solitary late-night jogger on the bike path which followed the waterway all the way to the beach. With dawning horror, I recollected just how easy it would have been for Jessica to walk along the bike path to Ratchett's unobserved. That would explain the absence of any other vehicle there the day I discovered his body. Fear clutched my heart. I was careening along the freeway on top of a vehicle driven by a murderer.

Suddenly the off-ramp sign announcing "Animal Shelter" loomed large in my line of vision. I tightened my grip and dug my toes in under the luggage rail as Jessica swerved right to exit, turned a hard left against a red light, then slowed as she approached the shelter. She parked, not in the shelter parking lot, vacant now except for a couple of employee vehicles and an animal control truck, but in the shopping center across the street, where she probably thought the Winnebago would be less conspicuous if someone from the shelter should happen to look out.

As soon as she set off across the street I made my way down the ladder. Whether I was more concerned that Jessica or a passing police car would spot me would be hard to determine. If riding on top of an RV wasn't an infraction of the California traffic code, the breaking and entering of one surely was.

As I reached the ground my legs were trembling from the tension of holding them taut for the past fifteen minutes. I caught sight of myself in the motor home's large side mirror. What a sketch! Hair standing on end, face and clothes smudged with dirt from the top of the RV. It was not a pretty sight. My white jeans and blue shirt, so very sharp-looking when I left home early that morning, had lost much of their sparkle, and so had I.

I now had a decision to make. I could continue my efforts to break into the motor home and release the dogs— rather risky as I was now in full view of a busy street—or I could follow Jessica and find out what she was up to. If

I went for help, she and the dogs might well be gone before it arrived.

Perhaps I should try to disable the motor home first? Decidedly not my area of expertise. Four wheels that go round is about all I know, or care to know, about cars. But I figured that if I could get into the cab, there might be a chance I could break something or pull a couple of wires loose. I tried the door, hoping to find it unlocked. But no luck. I would have to go with my second option.

Watson and Chamois were secure as long as they remained locked in the RV, and if Jessica returned I would be hard on her heels, I reasoned, as I decided to follow her.

By now both dogs were barking loudly. Watson knew I was there and was trying her best to communicate with me. Chamois, responding to instincts hitherto unplumbed, joined in uncertainly, surprising himself, no doubt, with a high-pitched yowl he had never before found it necessary to exercise.

I looked at my watch in the dim glow of the streetlights. I could just make out half past twelve. The night gate attendant would have left thirty minutes ago. The only person on duty at this hour would be the night dispatcher, probably passing the slow midnight to early morning hours dozing or listening to the radio inside the office building. There was seldom much for him to do at night, though someone was always on duty in case of an emergency.

Using the motor home to shield myself from view, I watched Jessica cross the street. Illuminated by the shelter parking lot lights, I could see that she had changed her long skirt and frilly blouse for a more practical sweat suit.

Halfway across the street she stopped in her tracks, turned, and headed back to the RV. Had she seen me? I ducked down under the motor home, bumping my head on the spare wheel as I did so. I held my breath. She unlocked the door, reached in, and took a large shoulder bag from the passenger seat, muttered a stern ''Be quiet!'' to the dogs, and set off again across the street.

What was she going to do? Ring the night bell and demand her dog back? That would be interesting. No way a dog would be released after hours.

But instead of ringing the bell, bold as brass she reached through the metal bars of the gate and undid the padlock. Of course. She had worked here; either she never turned in her master key, or she'd had a copy made during that time.

As soon as she entered the shelter, I crossed the street. She had not reclosed the padlock, and the gate yielded to a gentle push. Thinking to delay her getaway, I quietly clicked the padlock home, realizing too late that I had also cut off my own line of escape.

The shelter at night presented a quite different picture to that of the daytime. No busy kennel attendants; no anxious owners looking for lost pets. The sounds from the freeway, unnoticed during the day over the noise of barking, now dominated. A shelter that houses up to two hundred animals can never be entirely silent. Occasionally a dog would start barking for no apparent reason, then others would join in. Jessica would have little fear that barking dogs would arouse someone's curiosity.

She headed straight for the section where I had seen Herbie earlier. I followed at a discreet distance, so intent on keeping my eye on her that at one point I tripped over a hose which had been left lying across the walkway, setting off a minor chorus of yapping. Tails wagged as I put my fingers to my mouth and silently shushed.

I continued on to Herbie's run. There was no sign of Jessica. I thought Herbie seemed overly pleased to see me, until I realized he was looking past me. I turned and was hit by a powerful smack in the face.

Now I wished I'd taken that martial arts class I'd long procrastinated about. I tried to defend myself, but Jessica, amazingly agile for her size, had the advantage of surprise as well as height and weight. Before I could regain my feet, she had my wrists tied together behind my back with a nylon cord leash she had produced from her shoulder bag, along with a roll of duct tape.

Kicking out, I shouted for help. But my shouts were lost in a major crescendo of barking from the large dogs in the adjoining runs.

"Mrs. Doolittle," growled Jessica. "You let me down. I told you Herbie was not to come to the shelter."

"Does this mean I don't get the bonus?" was all I had time to say before the tape was slapped over my mouth.

. 30 .

The Scent of Death

WITH A LAST rueful look at Herbie, Jessica dragged me toward station four. Shouldering open the clinic door she shoved me inside, pushing the door shut behind her with her foot. She turned on the light, then grabbed a bunch of leashes from several hanging on the back of the door. Dumping me into a chair, one of those hideous institutional things, all wood and cracked leatherette, with stuffing protruding from the seat, she bound one leash across my chest and used two more to anchor my ankles. Nothing James Bond couldn't have escaped from in a second, surely.

But I was no James Bond. Right now I wasn't even sure I was Delilah Doolittle. The events of the past few hours were unlike any I had ever experienced before in my life. For the second time that day, I felt a now all-too-familiar prickle of fear.

The small room was typical of veterinary offices, with an examining table, twin sinks, the chair, a wheeled stool, and two supply cabinets, one on either side of a frosted glass window. What made this room different was the unusual odour, a strong scent of disinfectant, of course, but overlaid with the scent of death. It was coming from a steel barrel standing in the corner. Empty now, but filled daily with a deadly quota. Freeing animals from suffering and rejection was the main business of this room.

It was much quieter in here, the only noise the humming of the air conditioner and the mournful howling of one lonely dog protesting his fate. But for the tape across my mouth I would have howled mine, too, though I doubted my shouts would excite any more interest than the howls of the dog. The night dispatcher's office was at the other end of the building, and I was sure that he, like all shelter employees, had long since learned to tune out such noises.

I watched mutely as Jessica, her usually bland face grim and determined, unlocked the supply cabinet and sorted around until she found what she was looking for, assembling the items carefully in a plastic tray.

"You little busybody, following me here," she said. If only she knew! "It was a big mistake hiring you," she continued. "But before I finish you off, I need to know just exactly how much you've found out." She snatched the tape from my mouth, and I tasted blood on my lower lip.

If what I knew was that important to her, then I had to convince her that I knew more than I actually did, in hopes of prolonging the conversation until help arrived. If it arrived.

What would Mallory make of my message? If he was still of the opinion that my investigation had no bearing on his, he might fail to see its relevance. I cursed myself for not being more specific.

"Well, I know about the—"

I was interrupted by the ringing of the phone on the wall. Probably a wrong number, since normally no one would be in the clinic at this hour. Unless—was it possible the night dispatch man had seen the light go on in here and was calling to see who it was? We watched the light flashing several times, until the ringing finally stopped. In the silence the rings seemed to echo around the cheerless room. I prayed that it had been the night man, and he would come along to investigate.

"The body in the doghouse." Jessica picked up the conversation where we had left off. "Yes, of course you do. I hadn't expected you to search the house and grounds so thoroughly. I had planned to be long gone before that was found."

"Then you knew?" I was unable to hide my astonishment. Despite the fact that the evidence had been mounting throughout the day, I was still reluctant to believe that this proud, accomplished woman was capable of killing anyone.

"Of course," she replied. "Who do you think put him there?"

"You? But why?"

"Steven was a mistake." Jessica was so matter-of-fact, almost detached, in her recounting of how it all went wrong. It gave me chills. "It was supposed to be Jim Ratchett. I had asked him to take care of the dogs while I was in San Diego. He'd done it before, and it was in his interest to look after my affairs." Her eyes widened conspiratorially behind her bifocals, as if I was privy to this information. I nodded knowingly. Whatever it was she thought I knew, it was to my advantage to play along.

"I left him plenty of his favourite Jack Daniels so he'd relax, maybe even pass out," she continued. "But something went wrong. He sent his nephew instead. In the dark, I mistook Steven for his uncle." I remembered noticing in the photo Debbie had shown me how similar in stature Steven and Jim Ratchett had been.

As she talked she fingered her earrings, almost deliberately, it seemed, inviting me to look at them. I saw to my dismay that they were the jointed German shepherd ones. She must have discovered the missing piece after I left. Catching me staring at them, she said, "Thank you for retrieving that broken piece for me. These earrings have great sentimental value." Again, that odd sly look she'd given me in the kitchen earlier. She knew I knew!

That realization was confirmed by her next words. "But that's your problem, Mrs. Doolittle. You're too clever for your own good. When I realized how much you knew, I could delay my plans no longer. I had to come for Herbie tonight. It's too bad you followed me. You leave me no choice.''

Turning her attention to the tray on the counter, she picked up a syringe and with practiced movements filled it from a vial of sodium pentobarbital. A light sweat had broken out on her upper lip. She must be hot with that sweat jacket zippered to the throat.

She towered over me, and for the first time it hit me that she was really going to kill me.

"You're so fond of dogs and the shelter," she sneered, "you won't mind going the same way. Recycled into fertilizer, maybe. Or cosmetics, even pet food.''

I thought of the hundreds of unwanted animals that had met their end in this room. I was in no hurry to join them. And certainly not as fertilizer. That gave new meaning to the phrase "pushing up daisies.''

"Oh, get over yourself, Jessica," I said with more assurance than I actually felt. "They'll find me.''

"They'll never find you." She nodded in the direction of the barrel. "You're small enough to fit very neatly in there. Seal the lid, and no one will ever know the difference. The truck from the rendering company will pick you up in the morning, and you'll have vanished without a trace.''

"But they'll guess it was you who took Herbie, and they'll come after you.''

"By that time I'll be long gone. The motor home has enough supplies to last for months. All they'll know is a dog has been stolen, and if they do suspect me, well, how far are they going to chase a stolen dog? Into another state? I very much doubt it.''

The woman had quite taken leave of her senses. Though she spoke with confidence, I was sure it was mostly bravado. How long had she had to think up this scheme? The whole plan seemed very ill-advised.

My hopes of rescue were becoming dimmer by the minute. I debated the wisdom of telling her I had alerted the police. It was risky. Far from scaring her off, it might just precipitate her into doing me in straightaway and clearing out before help arrived.

I was beginning to doubt the possibility of that ever happening when I became conscious that the solitary howling which had continued nonstop since we had entered the clinic had now become a chorus as, in response to the wailing of approaching police sirens, first one dog, then another picked up the call. Like wolves howling a message across the wilderness, they were letting me know that help was on the way!

. 31 .

All Is Revealed

WE BOTH STOPPED talking and listened, Jessica tensing, her eyes darting back and forth as she tried to figure her best course of action, I buoyed with hope at the prospect of deliverance. But the sirens gradually faded and the howling subsided as the police continued on their quest on quite another matter. Tears pricked my eyes as I slumped in my chair with disappointment. Jessica, with a sigh of relief, turned to me with syringe in hand.

The false alarm had obviously distressed her. She was becoming more and more agitated. Red spots appeared on her normally pale cheeks. I wondered about blood pressure. I wished she would calm down. If she did carry out her threat the best I could hope for was that she would be swift and efficient, and not botch the job.

"Wait," I said. "Before I depart this earth, at least do me the courtesy of explaining how you managed to kill poor Steven when you were supposed to be in San Diego?"

"How could I be in two places at once?" Head up, chin thrust forward, she seemed almost to be seeking confirmation of the excellence of her scheme. "Simple. I begged off attending the best in group dinner, claiming I had a migraine. Then while everyone was at dinner, I took the trolley to the Santa Fe station and caught the eight-forty-five train back to Surf City.''

Of course. The one thing I couldn't figure out had been under my nose the whole time. Everything had fitted except I was so sure that Jessica was in San Diego when Steven was murdered. Now I remembered going through the stack of magazines and coming across the train schedule that first evening at Jessica's. And I'd had an identical schedule in my purse the whole time.

Jessica continued: "I got back to town, picked up my car from the station yard where I had left it earlier, and drove home. Ratchett, as I thought, was sitting in the living room watching television. I could smell the alcohol as soon as I walked through the door. He didn't even hear me come in.''

She picked up a piece of rubber tubing from the counter and proceeded to tie off a vein in my arm. Where was Mallory?

"My dogs didn't bark," she was saying. "They knew it was me. And they were confined to the dog run, as I had instructed. That's why I didn't realize Herbie was missing until I returned home at the weekend.''

With the back of her wrist she dabbed at the sweat on her upper lip, then continued: "I choked Ratchett—Steven, as it turned out—with one of those collars like he used for field training. I dragged him to the doghouse, returned to the house, switched off the lights and the television, and drove back to the station, just in time to catch the last train to San Diego. By the time I arrived the trolleys had stopped running, so I walked back to the park. It was late. Most of the lights were out in the RVs. But if anyone had seen me I would simply have said I was out getting some air after my sick headache.

"It was all working perfectly," she went on. "It was only after I got back home that things started to go wrong. First of all, Herbie had disappeared. Then you had to discover the body in the doghouse.'' She turned her fierce gaze on me.

I remembered how dumbstruck Jessica had appeared when we had found poor Steven. Understandably so, I had thought at the time. Disconcerting enough to find a body in one's doghouse. How much more disconcerting to discover the wrong body.

"Then Jim Ratchett started to get suspicious,'' she continued. "And I had to finish what I had started. And I would have finished you off, too, little miss busybody, if the police hadn't arrived.''

I wished she would stop calling me that. It was most irritating.

She had lost all her customary dignity and decorum. Gone was her habitual self-control, leaving in its stead a desperate woman, destroyed by her own pride and circumstances from which there was no extricating herself. I might have found it in my heart to pity her if my own situation hadn't been in extremis. My only hope was to keep her talking until help arrived. She seemed to find relief in relating what had happened. I played on that as I fought down my fear.

"And the notes, the house, Watson, Chamois? That was you?'' I asked.

"I was trying to get you to back off. Your dog put up quite a fight.'' She laid the syringe back down on the counter while she examined a deep scratch mark on her arm. "But the little Maltese. Your featherbrained friend practically gave me the dog,'' she said with a sneer. "I had followed you to the Mercedes dealer, and when she transferred her things from your car, she left the dog's carrier on the sidewalk. While you two were arguing in the showroom I simply picked up the bag and walked away.''

I recalled how annoyed Evie had been with me about her disastrous visit, culminating in her altercation with Officer Offley, and how I had tried to reason with her before she left in a huff.

I fidgeted in my seat; the stiff torn leatherette was sticking into my thighs, the rough corded leash was beginning to chafe my wrists, and I had pins and needles in my legs.

"But why hire me at all?" I said.

"When I realized Herbie was gone, I needed help to get him back before he got picked up by animal control," Jessica replied. "I couldn't leave town without him. I had heard that you had a reputation for finding lost pets quickly. But instead you had to turn what should have been a simple lost dog case into a police investigation," she finished angrily, jabbing an accusing forefinger at me.

Right. It was all my fault. I didn't let on that Steven Potter had stolen the dog in the first place, which really had thrown me off the track. It would only get her even more upset, and I had more questions. So far I only knew the who and the how.

She picked up the syringe again. I was running out of time.

"Hang on a tick," I said. "One more thing. Why did you have to kill Jim Ratchett in the first place?"

An almost maniacal gleam lit her pale green eyes, as she upended the syringe and expertly removed the bubbles with a flick of her forefinger.

"He was threatening to expose me. He had been at the shelter the day I adopted Herbie. He knew . . ." She checked herself, as if she had said more than enough.

But I could guess the rest: Ratchett knew Herbie had been a replacement for a beloved dog that had died. I recalled the box containing ashes on Jessica's mantelpiece, a picture of a dog identical to Herbie on its lid. Despite my predicament I empathized with how she must have felt that day, adopting Herbie in similar circumstances to the way in which I had obtained Watson—racing Ratchett to the office to save the dog from the junkyard.

Watson. What would become of her? And poor little Chamois? Evie would never forgive me.

Jessica took a firm grip on my arm and prepared to insert the syringe.

My number was up.

A screeching crash of metal against metal, soon followed by the smashing of glass, stilled the syringe in midair. Human voices joined a cacophony of barking as the door burst open.

"Gawd 'elp us," said Tony, surveying the unlikely scene.

"Oh, there you are, dear!" said Evie, seemingly quite unruffled.

Was I already in doggie heaven, or did she really have a gun in her hand?

32

Debriefing

"DON'T COME ANY closer," warned Jessica, the syringe already pressed against my arm.

As Evie hesitated in the doorway, there was a low growl, and a brown object streaked through the air. Watson, appearing suddenly from behind Tony, had lunged at Jessica, knocking her off balance. The gun fired inadvertently and an astonished Jessica fell slowly to her knees, then flat on her face with a thump. She was a very large lady. Blood seeped through the hip area of her sweatpants as the syringe rolled safely away into a corner.

Watson came over and placed her head in my lap.

"Gawd 'elp us," Tony said again.

"Oh, my God. Now look what you've made me do," shrieked Evie, glaring at me. "I've killed her." Her ample figure sausaged into a clingy red jumpsuit of lightweight wool, a gold lamé baseball cap covering her ash-blond, expensively dyed curls, she obviously considered herself suitably garbed for a caper.

"She'll come round soon enough. In handcuffs, I hope," said a voice from the door. Three pairs of eyes turned from dismayed regard of Jessica to the reassuring face of Mike Denver, who had arrived in time to hear Evie's cry of anguish. He took the tranquilizer gun from her trembling hands, and then went over and very carefully removed a three-and-a-half-inch dart from Jessica's hip.

Tony untied me, then used the leashes to secure the unconscious Jessica's hands and feet.

"You didn't 'alf give us a scare, luv," he said to me, his grey eyes full of concern.

To his usual attire of shorts, tee shirt, and sheepskin boots, Tony had now seen fit to add an Australian bush hat which, perched rakishly over one eye, had the curious effect, to my dazed eyes at least, of making him appear more the aging elf than ever.

He saw me eyeing the hat and, regaining his customary sense of humour, said, "As my old dad used to say, 'If you can't fight, wear a big 'at.' " He pushed up the brim with his thumb.

That lightened the mood, and everyone started talking at once.

Shock, then relief, had made Evie cross. "Dee, you are the absolute limit," she scolded.

Tony, meanwhile, hastened to absolve himself of any blame for the broken gun cabinet, while Mike attempted to get a handle on what had been happening at his shelter.

"There's going to be hell to pay when I find out who put that tranq. gun away fully charged," he said. He explained that the gun had been readied for an attempt to capture a coyote that had been raiding neighbourhood backyards, but that the search had been called off. "Fortunately, a coyote is only half that woman's weight, or the dosage might have killed her," he said.

The silence that followed while we pondered that sobering thought was broken by a new chorus of howling, as once again the shelter inmates heralded the approach of the police. This time the sirens ceased where they were supposed to—at the shelter parking lot.

With the arrival of Detective Mallory and Officer Offley, the small clinic had reached capacity. Mallory quickly took in the scene, then, turning to Mike, said, "Do you have a room where I can talk to these people and get their statements?"

Mike suggested the shelter's briefing room.

Evie had calmed down and, in a rare show of concern for someone other than herself, had dampened a paper towel at the sink and was attempting to clean up the cuts on my face.

Watching her, Mallory said, "That was a close call, Mrs. Doolittle." He looked stern, but his voice softened somewhat as he shook his head, saying, "I tried to warn you."

Offley, meanwhile, was assisting a groggy Jessica to her feet, handcuffing her and leading her away. "Jessica Lomax, you are under arrest for the murder of Steven Potter and James Ratchett. Anything you say . . ." he intoned as they went down the hallway and out toward the main gate. Mallory followed them out.

Mike led the rest of us along a corridor, past offices variously labeled Licensing, Field Services, Veterinarian, all empty now in the predawn hours, to the briefing room, a large work-worn area where the animal control officers received their daily assignments. Several rows of chairs faced a podium and a blackboard. On one wall a large notice board held work rosters, training class information, a vacation schedule, and a variety of animal-related cartoons clipped from newspapers and magazines. Another wall held a large street map of the city, neatly dissected into animal control precincts.

From the adjoining dispatch office, radio static reported a traffic accident involving a deer on the highway out by the Cleveland National Forest. As the world comes awake, traffic increases and wildlife will lie low if it knows what's good for it.

While we waited for Mallory, Tony filled me in on how he and Evie had found me. "When I went to see if Watson had come home, like you asked, I found Mrs. C., 'ere," ("Evie, dear boy," she murmured) "waiting for you."

Evie took up the story. "I had driven back to San Clemente to see if I could find any trace of Chamois," she said. "I called home from there to see if there was any news from you, got your message, and, of course, came straight on. Tony and I compared notes and decided to follow you to Jessica's."

"I twigged where you'd gone," put in Tony. "You should've waited for the police. But you were in too much of a bloody 'urry, as usual."

"Let me finish, dear boy," Evie interrupted. "Finding no one there, we were on the way back to your place when, going past the shelter, the dear boy spotted Jessica's motor home."

"Recognized it from the spare wheel cover, didn't I?" the dear boy put in.

On investigation they had found Watson and Chamois. It had been Tony's idea to bring Watson along in the hope that she could pick up my scent and lead them to me.

"Thank heavens you did," I said, petting Watson, sitting as if glued to my side, her head in my lap.

They had rung the night bell for a good ten minutes before, unable to rouse anyone, they had, in desperation, crashed Tony's precious vintage woody through the gate.

"How noble of you, Tony," I said gratefully.

They had seen the lights in the clinic, and made their way there, stopping only long enough to break open the gun cabinet and pick up the tranquilizer gun.

I was still trying to comprehend the unlikely duo of Tony and Evie joining forces to come to my rescue, when Mike came in with coffee. If there is one thing I cannot abide it is a hot drink in a plastic cup, but I refrained from saying so. I didn't want to hurt Mike's feelings. Evie, however, had no such scruples.

"Don't you have any china cups, young man?" she asked him. Tony almost choked on his coffee, while Mike just shook his head in bemusement. His expression indicated he'd never come across the likes of Evie before.

Regaining his composure, Mike told us he had been called in by the night dispatch man, who had become concerned when there was no response to his telephone call to the clinic. He was opening the back gate for Mike while Tony and Evie were attempting to gain entry at the front.

"I'm gasping for a ciggie," said Evie, studiously ignoring the "no smoking" sign and delving into her copious gold leather designer shoulder bag. She placed her cigarette into a slender gold holder, lighting it from a tiny gold and diamond lighter, manipulating carefully to avoid damaging her elegantly manicured crimson nails.

"Gawd, I don't know how you can smoke them things," Tony said in disgust.

"I'll have you know these are the best British imports," she retorted.

"That's what I mean," he said. "Twice as strong and deadly as American fags. Coffin nails I calls 'em."

When Mallory joined us it appeared he had decided to dispense with the usual procedure and was prepared for an informal exchange of information.

I gathered he had not been idling away the time doing crossword puzzles while I solved his case for him.

Jessica had not become a prime suspect until after Ratchett was murdered, he told us. "When I found out that Steven Potter was a last-minute replacement for Ratchett, it got me wondering if Ratchett hadn't been the intended victim all along."

Checking Jessica's San Diego alibi he learned that no one recalled seeing her after the best in group judging the day of Potter's murder. "She wasn't seen again until the early hours of the following morning, when one of the competitors, out for an early jog with her greyhounds, recalled seeing her walking in the show grounds. But there was the problem of opportunity. How could she have been in two places at once?"

Turning to me, Mallory said, "You tipped me off to the train possibility when you mentioned you'd been to San

Diego to help your friend find her dog, and had returned home again so quickly."

"Chamois," screeched Evie. "Where's Chamois?"

"Calm down, luv," said Tony. "He's locked up safe and sound in my car, along with Trix. Remember?"

Other than a mild raising of eyebrows, Mallory ignored the interruption, continuing, "Then on checking Ratchett's bank records we discovered he had been receiving a regular payment of a thousand dollars from Jessica for the last eight months."

I gasped. "Maybe that's why the house was up for sale!"

Mallory nodded. "Possibly she was running low on funds. What I still haven't figured out, though, is why he was blackmailing her. I guess the answer to that will have to wait until we question her."

"I think I can explain," I said, "from something Jessica said tonight. Ratchett knew Jessica had obtained Herbie from the shelter. He was there the day she adopted him. After the dog himself for his wretched guard dog business, no doubt. Once he found out that she was passing the dog off as a champion, he could have threatened to tell people that the dog had no authentic pedigree, that Herbie's pups were not from a champion line, as she claimed. Then her reputation, her life's work, would have been at stake."

"I see," said Tony. "Then if Ratchett figured out Jessica had killed Steven, maybe he upped the ante on the blackmailing, threatening to go to the police."

"But what difference would it make where this dog Herbie came from?" asked Evie, looking around for an ashtray, then flicking the ash on the floor.

"He was a ringer for a champion dog that had died," I said. "I'm guessing Jessica simply used the dead dog's pedigree for Herbie. I've been told there's no sure way to authenticate a dog's papers. That's why she was paranoid about keeping Herbie out of the shelter where she knew they scanned for microchips. If there was any dispute, the microchip would be proof that this was not Jessica's dog originally.''

"But . . . murder?'' Evie said with a shudder.

"Pride,'' I answered. "The threat of discovery put her over the edge. She couldn't bear to have people find out her reputation was built on a lie. Her champion dog, the one she had hoped would take best of breed at Madison Square Garden, had died. In Herbie she saw a chance to continue the dream.''

"Well, more than her reputation's destroyed now,'' Mallory said dryly.

"What about the electronic collars?'' asked Tony. "Surely she didn't think they were powerful enough to kill.''

"She asked me once if something couldn't be done about the use of those collars,'' put in Mike. "I told her no, that they were perfectly safe when used correctly. But she wasn't convinced, and said Ratchett deserved a taste of his own treatment.''

"Maybe it was her idea of poetic justice,'' I mused.

Mallory told us that he had traced the collars to a wholesale supplier in Los Angeles who had provided a short list of local customers, Jim Ratchett and Jessica Lomax among them. He was on his way to interview Jessica when he'd received my message. He had seen my car parked in the street near her house, but no sign of either of us. Then a bulletin came over his car radio of a possible break-in at the shelter.

"Putting it together with your confusing message about Jessica's dog at the shelter, well, you know the rest.'' Mallory closed his notebook, then looked me straight in the eye and said, "Take my advice, Mrs. Doolittle. Never take up a life of crime. You leave a trail a blind man could follow.''

He pushed back his chair, indicating that the interview was over. "Mrs. Doolittle, Mrs. Cavendish, Mr. Tipton, we'll need signed statements from each of you. We'll be in touch.''

As he turned to leave the room, Mallory said to me, "You should go to the emergency room and get those bruises and cuts looked at." His brusque manner belied the concern in his blue-grey eyes.

"No really. I'm fine," I protested. "Nothing that a good night's rest won't cure."

As the door closed behind him, Tony gave me a playful nudge in the ribs. " 'Ere, I think he fancies you," he said, an impish grin spreading over his tanned, lined face.

My cheeks burned. "I look such a sketch, how could he resist?" I retorted to cover my embarrassment. Tony said no more, just gave me a knowing and very annoying wink.

Evie, however, had plenty to say. "Don't be foolish, dear boy. I have quite other plans for Delilah."

I had no idea what or who she had in mind, but I devoutly hoped that her "other plans" did not involve Tennis Ted.

· 33 ·

Tailpiece

"HOW PRETTY," EVIE was saying. "What kind of a sky do you call that?"

"Sunrise," replied Tony and I in unison.

"Oh, of course," she said, not in the least disconcerted. It was probably many years since Evie had been up and about this early, and it would undoubtedly be many more before she was up and about this early again, and she didn't care who knew it.

"Well, it's too bad it can't occur later in the day when more people could enjoy it," she said.

Lack of sleep and all the excitement must have made her light-headed. I myself was feeling quite done in by the harrowing events of the previous night.

We were on the way home in my car, Tony's cherished woody having been towed away for some serious body-work, which I had an uneasy feeling I ought to pay for. With little hope of getting paid by Jessica, this had turned out to be a most expensive undertaking.

On learning that Major and Sheba and the two cats were at Jessica's house unattended, Mike had assigned a truck to go over and pick them up, and had allowed us, dogs and all, to hitch a ride to pick up my car.

As far as her pets were concerned, Jessica had two options: if she got out on bail, she could claim them herself. If she didn't make bail, she could either designate someone to care for them during her absence, which might well extend beyond several dog lifetimes, or she could release them for adoption. I made a mental note to alert the German shepherd rescue people that the shelter might soon have some good-looking dogs for adoption. I might even take Herbie myself.

Not today though. We had an abundance of dogs already—five in fact. Watson, Chamois, and Trixie, of course. Then Tasha. I had forgotten all about Mrs. Jones' poodle until she yapped with joy when she saw me walking through the shelter on my way to the gate, and I remembered with compunction that I had never called Mrs. Jones after I had spotted the dog the previous afternoon. The business with Jessica had quite put it out of my head.

I persuaded Rita, who had come into work early after the report of the break-in, to open up the office before business hours so that I could retrieve Tasha and return her to Mrs. Jones as soon as possible.

Then, just as we were passing adoption row on our way out, a particular bark over and above the rest attracted my attention.

"Oh, no!" I said.

"What now?" said Evie.

"It's the Brittany spaniel I told you about. The one that flunked hunting 101."

Rita, who was walking us to the gate, explained that after the dogs from Ratchett's kennel were impounded, the owners of those animals boarded for training had been contacted by telephone. Most of them had already picked up their dogs. But the Brittany's owner had come in and signed her off, Ratchett having reported earlier that she wasn't responding well to field training. We stared in dismay at the dog whose only crime had been that she was too sensitive for Jim Ratchett's harsh training methods.

Finally, Evie said, "I'll take her. I'll give her to Howard for his birthday. A sporting dog is just what he needs to complete his outdoorsman image. He'll be thrilled."

"But she can't hunt," I said dubiously, not wanting to talk Evie out of giving the dog a home but reluctant to see Howard saddled with a useless dog.

"Neither can Howard," she said airily. "I won't allow it. They'll be well-matched."

The Brittany, now sitting on the front seat between us, was sorely in need of a bath after being penned up for several days. Dirty paw prints on car upholstery were all in a day's work to me, but they would certainly tend to diminish the luster of Evie's spanking new Mercedes.

Chamois sat in Evie's lap in quiet bemusement, blissfully unaware that the Brittany, already nuzzling possessively alongside his mistress, was soon to be sharing his space permanently. His barrette vanished, hair in eyes, and in sore need of a good brushing, Chamois looked like I felt.

Tony was in the back with Trixie, Watson, and Tasha. Watson sat behind me, her head resting on my shoulder, determined not to be separated from me again, and meanwhile watching the road ahead, as intently as any backseat driver. Trixie and Tasha bounded about excitedly, giving new meaning to the words perpetual motion.

"Keep a firm grip on Tasha," I warned Tony. "She's an escape artist."

It was with relief that we delivered the hyper poodle to her home. A surprised and delighted Mrs. Jones came to the door in curlers and bathrobe. "Oh, there you are, you naughty girl," she said, taking the wriggling runaway from my grasp. "Say thank you to Delilah for finding you again." Tasha ran indoors with never a backward glance.

Reaching home, we sorted out dogs and owners. Evie and Tony both had the decency to refuse my offer to come in for a cup of tea. Tony was eager to get to the beach and check out the waves.

Evie, too, was anxious to be on her way. Britt, as the

spaniel had been promptly named, hopped into the front seat of the Mercedes as to the manor born. I hoped she would be a pleasant surprise, not a nasty shock for Howard. But, a reluctant retriever for a specious sportsman? It might work at that.

Chamois was confined once more to his sport bag, which Evie leashed securely to the passenger seat belt. She was taking no more chances.

"Dear boy." Evie reached out of her car window and patted Tony's arm as they said their adieus. "You must come to dinner next time you're in San Diego. I will be quite put out if you don't. You and Howard have so much in common." Other than a high tolerance for silliness, I could not for the life of me think of a thing.

Squelching this thought as uncharitable, I waved goodbye thankfully, and with Watson padding along beside me, went indoors.

Walking by my desk I noticed the red light on the answering machine flashing madly. The first message was Rita's from yesterday, telling me about the shepherd that had just come in. As for the rest:

Beep: "*There's a peacock on my roof and it won't go away. It's making a terrible noise.*"

Beep: "*Please tell me what I should do about the family of possums in my bathtub.*"

Beep: "*There's a skunk under my deck. How do I get rid of it?*"

Peacocks on the roof, opossums in the bathtub, skunks under the deck. And, no doubt, bats in the belfry, given time. They would all keep for another day. As I reached over to disconnect the phone, an old blue teddy bear was dropped at my feet.

Watson wanted to play.